Books by J

The Nephilim Series
Demons and Angels
The Night Everything Fell Apart

The Druids of Avalon series
Celtic Fire
The Grail King
Deep Magic
Silver Silence

Immortals series
The Awakening
The Crossing
Blood Debt

also by Joy Nash
A Little Light Magic
Christmas Unplugged
Looking for a Hero

www.joynash.com

Praise for Joy Nash

Silver Silence

"Spellbinding! Joy Nash combines her knowledge of Celtic lore with timeless legends and writes breathtaking romance of unconditional love amid a backdrop of lush descriptions and powerful magic." ~*Paranormal Romance Reviews*

The Grail King

A Romantic Times TOP PICK! "Not since Mary Stewart's *Merlin Trilogy* has the magic of Avalon flowed as lyrically off the pages." ~*RT BOOKreviews Magazine*

A Little Light Magic

"One of those books that when you finish reading it, you have to turn around and start it all over again." ~*Bitten by Books*

The Crossing

"Splendidly entertaining." ~*Booklist* on *The Crossing*
"Mac's personality is in full blaze. It is impossible not to fall in love with this man!" ~*Romance Junkies*

Looking For a Hero

"Oh man! A hilarious ride that had me falling out of my seat with laughter... Don't miss this story." ~*Romance Reviews Today*

Blood Debt

An Immortals Novel

Joy Nash

JOYNASH BOOKS LLC
Doylestown PA

Blood Debt
An Immortals Novel
Copyright © 2013 by Joy Nash
ISBN-13: 978-1-941017-04-3
Published by: joynash books, llc
Doylestown PA, USA
Cover design by Story Wonk
Interior design by Joy Nash

All Rights Reserved.

This is a work of fiction. Names, characters, places, and incidents are either products of the author's imagination or are used fictitiously and are not to be construed as real. Any resemblance to actual names or persons, living or dead, or to places, events, organizations, business establishments, events or locales, is entirely coincidental.

First Paperback Edition: November 2016

To second chances

Chapter One

Rome, Italy.

The Eternal City.

When all was said and done, it was a fitting place for a vampire.

Arthur Jackson Cabot IV swirled the ruby contents of his wineglass. The heat of the day lingered in the iron of the balcony rail, but somehow the warmth did not transfer to his bare forearms.

The sun was gone. From his hotel's perch atop a lofty hill behind Vatican City, Jackson watched twilight sigh into surrender. Church domes faded into ink-dark sky. Wary lights winked to life, one by one, an offering spread at his feet.

Night had come.

Night. His refuge and his torment.

Hunger gnawed Jackson's gut. His hand shook, causing the red liquid in his glass to tremble. He rubbed his eyes against the sting left by the harsh lights suspended above the Colosseum more than three miles distant. He'd heard news of a charity concert in the ancient arena. A cadre of international rock stars raising money to aid vampire addicts—those unfortunate humans ensnared by the pleasures to be had in vampire clubs. They offered their blood and life essence to the undead in return for the mind-blowing high only a vampire bite could provide.

A passel of indulgent do-gooder millionaires prancing about on a stage thought they could save humans bent on their own destruction? Jackson's laugh was low and unamused.

The night was overly warm and humid. His linen shirt clung to his chest, glued to his skin by a sheen of sweat tainted by city pollution. Jackson shifted his shoulders, trying to dislodge a feeling of uncleanliness. But the fabric only clung that much more.

His throat burned. The sensation had advanced far beyond subtle irritation. It now approached unendurable pain. He couldn't ignore his thirst much longer, no matter how much he despised his craving. Summer bloodthirst was especially loathsome. Summer days were too long, summer nights too hot. Summer brought memories. It had been summer when death came for him.

Came, but had not completely succeeded in taking.

He peered into his glass. Contemplated taking a sip, then rejected the notion. With a subtle twist of his wrist, he poured the liquid over the balcony railing into the garden below. Call it an offering to a vengeful god.

A poor offering, at that. It was only wine, after all.

The balcony door scraped open.

"Monsieur Cabot?"

He closed his eyes. He wished to hell and back that his kind could exist in solitude. But it was impossible. A vampire required a human caretaker. One such as he couldn't sleep unprotected when the sun was high in the sky.

His steward's loyalty was yet another punishment. Solange was far too young for the thankless job she'd inherited from his previous steward, her grandfather. True, years ago Jackson had saved the man's life, but that debt had been repaid a thousandfold by now. If the tables had been turned, Jackson would have been long gone.

"Monsieur?" Solange ventured. "Are you...well?"

He turned. Silhouetted in the doorway, the young death witch met his gaze with steady purpose. Even as a child she'd been solemn. Lately, she'd been infinitely more so.

"Will you roam tonight?"

The question was offered with deference, but Solange's lowered eyes did not shield the worried cadence of her heart. Jackson could hear the organ beating swiftly against her ribs. The fingers of her right hand twisted the plain gold band on her left. So newly a bride, so newly bereft, and Jackson had been unable to prevent her loss. Another dark mark on his already black soul. Had only three months passed since Jean-Claude had been taken? It seemed like an eternity.

"The moon waxes," Solange said. "You must—"

He lifted a brow and she bit off the work with a flush of embarrassment. A steward did not command her master. At least, not directly.

"I am sorry, monsieur."

He handed her his glass. "Don't worry," he told her. "I do intend to drink tonight."

Relief rippled through her. "That is good."

"But I will not roam. The hotel can provide what I need."

"That too, is good." She stepped back through the balcony door. "Legrand's minions are sniffing about. The bastard knows you are here in Rome."

He followed her, his bare toes sinking into plush carpet.

"It is nothing I did not expect. The endgame approaches."

Her nostrils flared. "It is too soon. You cannot be certain you will win. Not yet. You should go into hiding. Until we are sure you are strong enough."

Jackson set his wineglass on the bar. The stem cracked under the pressure of his frustration. He'd waited years upon years. Now, with the end in sight, it was imperative not to lose patience. He must proceed with utmost care. But...

"How I wish I could end it all tonight."

He glanced toward the window, weighing the risk of such a rash action.

Solange's eyes widened. "No! I beg of you, no. It is not yet time. We must be careful. Legrand's vampires roam the night and his stewards hunt by day. It is foolish to linger in the open. Feed with haste and let us go to ground before the sun rises. You must not risk—"

He gave her a speaking glance.

She flushed but did not avert her eyes. "I apologize, monsieur, for my forward speech. But I am...concerned."

He did not deny that her concern was prudent. Solange may be young, but her instincts were excellent. Jackson wished he could ignore her advice. He did not want to leave this place so soon. The illusion of humanity he maintained as a guest in a human hotel was as potent as a lover's kiss. Pragmatism, alas, was a much less seductive mistress.

Ah, well. What he preferred was of no consequence. When it came to self-denial, Jackson was a master.

He inclined his head. "Thank you for your care. It will be as you wish. We depart one hour before dawn. Inform the others."

Solange gave him a fleeting smile before bending to retrieve his broken wine glass. "Very good. I will make the appropriate arrangements."

Jackson strode to his bedroom, stripped off his damp clothing, and dressed anew. When he returned to the sitting room Solange stood waiting, once again twisting her wedding ring. She wasn't aware of the habit, he thought. Or perhaps she was, but could not stop.

"There is a *fête* on the terrace," she informed him. "Wine flows and lovers stroll in the gardens beyond the swimming pool. Enzo and Gunter are already in attendance. You will easily find what you need there."

Jackson nodded, already heading toward the door. By now his craving had taken on an edge of desperation. The sensation displaced his guilt at what would come next.

His fangs elongated, cutting the inside of his lip. Blood touched his tongue. Stolen blood, its human life essence severely depleted. His throat felt raw.

His thirst burned.

Somehow he managed to turn, hand on the doorknob, and speak in a normal tone. "I won't be long. Don't wait up for me. Go to your room and get some sleep."

His steward inclined her head and Jackson entered the night.

***

Solange had been right, as she most often was. The party on the hotel terrace provided easy hunting. Enzo and Gunter roamed the edges of the glittering crowd. He watched as the pair laughed and exchanged shallow pleasantries with the guests. Each young vampire escorted a stunningly beautiful woman.

Jackson's eyes narrowed but he knew the living females would come to no permanent harm from his minions' feedings. Enzo and Gunter had served him for several decades and were well accustomed to Jackson's rules concerning restraint among living humans. Neither vampire would dare disobey their master's orders.

He plucked a wineglass from a tray, but did not drink. With calculated nonchalance, he strolled the terrace, mingling with the wealthy, multi-national revelers, switching from Italian to French to English with ease. His youthful lessons in language and deportment had proven useful, just as his blue-blooded Boston Brahmin grandmother had insisted they would. Of course, she'd never expected him to have a hundred years in which to perfect his accent.

The burning in his gut drove him to make his selection quickly. Females, all. Feeding on men unearthed memories best left buried. He lured his first victim into the lush greenery beyond the terrace. The vivacious Milanese model did not realize how close to danger she ventured. His first bite after a period of abstinence was always the most difficult to control. But he managed to lift his head after just three long sips.

She stumbled away, dazed. Immediately, he lured another victim. Blonde. British. Her escort's brow creased as she made her excuses and slipped away with the pallid stranger she'd just met.

And so the evening progressed, with sips from a dozen veins pulsing in a dozen slender necks. Life—intoxicating life—flooded Jackson's body. With life came lust, weighting and warming his loins. Exercising long-practiced willpower, Jackson denied his body's demand for sex. He closed each victim's wound and erased the pain from her mind, leaving only a vague impression of pleasure. Call it a payment of sorts. Yet Jackson felt every bit the dirty thief that he was.

A dainty female hand touched his arm. "*Voresti andare alla mia camera, signore?*"

Would you like to go to my room? The beautiful woman beside him pursed her red lips and blew him a kiss. Jackson's heart, pumping its stolen blood, thudded against his ribs.

This one had red hair.

His body clenched. Pure fire flowed into his erection. Several seconds passed before he trusted himself to voice a rejection. "*Mi dispiace, bella, ma no.*"

The woman pouted and departed with a huff of annoyance. Jackson stared at the luxurious auburn cascade until she disappeared into the crowd. He would wager the color was not natural. And still, he was tempted.

At last, sated with stolen blood, disgusted with himself, and aroused almost beyond bearing, Jackson all but fled to the elevator.

Solange had extinguished the lights in his suite. Jackson dropped onto the leather couch in front of a blank television screen. On his feet again within moments, he paced.

God in Heaven. That hair. Even though it had come from a bottle, it so nearly resembled—

His erection throbbed. Visions of the Italian redhead from the terrace—naked, lying on white satin, arms flung overhead—blended with the image of another auburn-haired siren. A beautiful Celtic Sidhe he'd not seen in a hundred years.

Striding to the bar, he passed over the wine in the decanter and opted for whiskey. He poured it, unwatered, down his throat. The tumbler cracked in his hand as he fought to master his breathing. At this rate, he would owe the hotel an entire new set of glassware.

He chanted a mantra. The soft syllables provided a measure of calm. He grasped at that elusive peace, tried to pull it inside him.

The urge to utter a prayer—for strength, for forgiveness—was all but overwhelming. He resisted it. An old Harvard drinking toast, proclaiming the superiority of the New World aristos that ruled their ivied halls, claimed the Boston Cabots talked only to God. Jackson had withdrawn from his ancestors' futile conversation long ago.

Slowly, surely, he mastered his demons, his memories, his painful lust. And was rewarded with a surge of power, drawn from his night's hunt. Life, health, immortality— they blazed through his veins in blinding glory, as bright as the sun he could no longer look upon.

A few moments later, his breathing was quiet, his body relaxed. It was at moments like this, soon after feeding, after the worst of the guilt had faded, that he felt almost human. He settled anew on the sofa, his long legs crossed and propped on the cocktail table in front of him. Absently, he picked up the remote and pointed it at the television.

He scanned several channels, then paused at live coverage of the Colosseum's charity concert. The international effort sported the usual collection of socially conscious musical superstars, both human and supernatural: Bono, Sting, Springsteen, McCartney, Manannán. A female reporter with luscious breasts discharged a rapid Italian commentary near the backstage entrance, where fifty or more hysterical females mobbed a line of police barriers, apparently waiting for the arrival of one of the night's acts.

He was about to change the channel when a sleek black limo, escorted by four *polizia* mounted on flag-adorned motorcycles, slowed before the ancient stone archway. Jackson lowered the remote as the limo door opened.

Out sprang Manannán mac Lir. The demigod musician's father was the Celtic god Lir; his mother was Niniane, Queen of the Sidhe. Manannán, however, seemed to prefer living in the human realms. His blend of traditional Celtic and modern electronic music had enjoyed a certain modest following for decades. Then, two years ago, the demigod had assisted the celebrated Immortal Warriors in saving the world from a crazed demon. Once that feat had become public, Manannán's musical popularity had exploded across the globe. Hysterical women everywhere—and not a few men, too—flung themselves at the handsome blond demigod with tedious unoriginality. Jackson wondered if Manannán took advantage of these human offerings. Last year it had been reported—incredibly—that he'd married a human death witch. Jackson couldn't imagine a Sidhe demigod stooping so low.

Tonight, Manannán greeted his adoring public with a wide grin and a friendly wave. Several figures spilled from the limo behind him. First came a pair of dark-haired human females. Manannán draped an arm around one of them, a happy, glowing woman who certainly did not have the somber look of a death witch. Tales of the demigod's bizarre marriage had most likely been fabricated to boost tabloid sales.

Next to alight was a very large, very disgruntled man wearing a tuxedo jacket and Scottish dress kilt. Jackson recognized him as the Immortal Kalen, hero to the human race and obscenely rich patron of the arts. Photos of Kalen and his Immortal Warrior brothers appeared regularly on the covers of celebrity rags and on Internet blogs. Jackson remembered seeing a photo of Kalen's immense castle, situated on an island off the northern coast of Scotland. Even Jackson, reclusive vampire that he was, couldn't escape the never-ending Immortals media hype.

Kalen moved to the side of the second woman, placing himself between her and the unruly crowd as Manannán turned and offered his free hand to the last occupant of the limo. Jackson found himself riveted by a pair of long, exquisite legs.

The rest of the woman emerged from the vehicle, piece by piece, like candy spilling from a bag. Shapely thighs.

Curvaceous hips. Tiny waist. Lush breasts. Slender neck. A beautiful profile.

Pointed Sidhe ears peeking through long, shining auburn hair.

"My God."

Abruptly, Jackson's feet slid off the table. They hit the ground with such force the flat television screen shook on its mounting. He gasped as his mind blanked on a rush of white-hot lust, followed closely by a wash of red-hot anger.

His cock hardened with painful intensity.

He stared at the screen. She passed under the ancient stone archway and out of the camera's view. One hundred years had passed since he'd last seen her. But it would take much longer than a mere century to erase this particular redhead from his mind.

He'd thought she'd be dead by now. Sidhe could live indefinitely, unless they met with an untimely accident or an enemy bent on murder. This particular Sidhe female was half human, more than likely to die in the normal course of events. And she'd surely collected enough enemies over the years who would be happy to see her dead.

At the very least, Jackson thought bitterly, she might have had the decency to age a decade or two. But no. She was as alive, as young, and as beautiful as he remembered.

And still consorting with artists, as she had all those years ago in Paris.

He'd worshiped this woman. In return, she'd whispered words of devotion, fucked him blind, and left him for dead. But Jackson hadn't died—or at least, not as completely as she'd expected.

It was a mistake she'd soon regret. Dearly.

He stood.

It seemed he was meant to roam tonight, after all.

Chapter Two

Leanna's handsome half-brother sent her a grin brilliant enough to charm an ogre from its den.

"Ah, come now, love, you can't mean to retire so early. The night's barely got started. The clubs are waiting." Pumped from his stage performance, Manannán mac Lir radiated more life energy than should be legal in the human world.

"Yes, but—" Leanna began.

"But nothing, little sister. Rome needs you."

Artemis, Mac's wife, rolled her eyes. "Listen, Mac, we can't stay out too long. I need to get back in time for Cameron's four a.m. feeding."

"Then we best get going quickly, no? Come now, Leanna. You can't let Artemis and me dance alone."

"I don't think—"

"Mac," Artemis broke in, "Can't you take a hint? Leanna doesn't want to go clubbing. Leave her be. You didn't say a word when Kalen and Christine left for the hotel after the last curtain call."

"Kalen's a bloody old man," Mac said without heat. "He hates crowds and Christine, bless her soul, thinks little Ellie will give Nanny Pearl too much of a fuss." He snorted. "As if there's anything that old biddy can't handle."

Leanna hid a smile. Kalen's mixed-blood Halfling/gnome housekeeper did have a special talent with children—even three such imps as Kalen and Christine's immortal daughter, Mac and Artemis's semi-divine firstborn, and Artemis's magically talented older son.

Mac's green eyes narrowed on Leanna. "What's wrong, love? You're always good for a late-night jaunt. Not ill, are you?"

"No, nothing like that. I'm just tired." And melancholy. "You and Artemis go on and have fun. I'll take a taxi back to the hotel."

"Not a chance. We'll have the limo drop you off. I've just got a few fans to greet at the back gate..."

A "few" fans turned into ten, then twenty. By the time Mac and Artemis dropped Leanna at their hotel at the top of the Spanish Steps, two a.m. had come and gone.

Muted voices and the strains of guitar drifted from a knot of tourists lingering on the famed Baroque stairway. Leanna didn't look over. She'd sat on those steps years ago, laughing and flirting with a young English poet named John Keats, in the shadow of the house where he'd died not long after.

Leanna had killed him.

Oh, all right, maybe technically it hadn't been murder. Leanna was a Celtic *leannan-sidhe*, or love muse. In a world neatly divided between life magic and death magic, Leanna was somewhat of an anomaly. Technically, she was a creature of life magic. But since her magic was inextricably linked with her sexuality, and since so many humans were willing to die to possess it, Leanna's life magic was, paradoxically, an instrument of human self-destruction.

Keats had surrendered his life of his own free will, just as all Leanna's doomed lovers had. Each desperate artist had lusted after the inspiration her sex magic could provide. To a man, each poet, painter, and musician had willingly traded his life essence for the fleeting fame he'd craved more than life itself.

How could it be Leanna's fault if the artists she'd been with had chosen to die? That's how Leanna had rationalized her muse magic for more than two hundred years. She couldn't lie anymore. Not even to herself. True, her lovers had been free to reject the magical inspiration she'd offered them. Then again, she was well able to engage in sex without casting her muse magic. She'd known full well that her lure was nearly irresistible to certain humans. In fact, she'd made a habit of choosing lovers who were likely to be the most susceptible.

Funny how a year in the death realms, enslaved by a demon, changed one's perspective on the issue of magical ethics. In Hell, there had been no hope: she'd been trapped, facing an eternity of death and darkness. The experience had stripped her of every illusion: she'd seen her earlier life as the perversion it had been, and had regretted it desperately. The worst of it had not been her own misery, but the knowledge that she'd never be able to make atonement to the many human lovers she'd destroyed.

It had been a pure miracle that Mac had stumbled upon Leanna in that horrible place. At the time, he'd been pursuing Artemis through the nine circles of Hell. He hadn't known—or cared, presumably—where Leanna was being held captive.

A second miracle had occurred when Mac had decided his half-sister's miserable arse was worth saving. She'd surely given him no reason to put himself at risk for her. Leanna had given Mac what assistance she could in Hell, but her actions had been little enough to make up for a past in which she'd tried her best to destroy her brother.

But Mac, ever quick to love, and even quicker to forgive, had saved her. Afterwards he'd gained her entrance to Annwyn, the Celtic Otherworld, the realm ruled by their mother, Queen Niniane. That had been the third miracle: Mac had managed to convince Niniane not only to acknowledge her mixed-breed daughter, but to allow Leanna to remain in Annwyn with Mac for the better part of a year. During that time, much of the damage Hell had done to both their souls had healed. Now Leanna and her brother were something she'd never dreamed they'd be. Friends.

Mac gave a final wave as his limo pulled away. Leanna drew a breath, but mere oxygen wasn't enough to fill the hollow sensation in her chest. In the past year since returning to the human world, Mac had conquered his inner demons, married his true love, and fathered a child. In contrast, Leanna had done...nothing. Nothing at all.

She neared the hotel's front desk. The night clerk was handsome and young, with olive skin and bedroom eyes. And he was, as fate would have it, an artist.

A sketchbook lay open before him and a pencil graced his elegant, long-fingered hand. The half-finished drawing, she noted with a practiced eye, showed the beginnings of true brilliance. The clerk looked up from his work, greeting her with an innocent smile. Before she quite knew what she was doing, a tendril of her muse magic escaped and floated towards him.

Its caress caused him to go still. His pupils darkened and he swallowed thickly. Leanna had no doubt that hidden behind the desk, his cock was thickening as well.

Gods. How long had it been since she'd slept with an artist? More than two long years. The ugly truth was, Leanna missed her muse magic. The heady exchange of inspiration and life, delivered at the precise moment of orgasm, was a mind-blowing high, one she'd reveled in for two centuries while her conscience slept.

Right here, right now, she wanted this boy, fiercely. She could lose herself in him, at least for one night. It wouldn't be a one-sided exchange. There was much she could offer him. She could give him his fondest dream. Under the influence of her magic he would create magnificent works of art. His fame would be instant. The world would throw itself at his feet and worship him as a god.

But not before he'd exchanged every drop of his life essence for Leanna's inspiration. In the end, the world would mourn another tragic, youthful death of a brilliant artist who'd had so much to live for.

Leanna yanked her magic back just in time. What had she been thinking? She couldn't invite this young man to bed, no matter how lonely she was. He could very well be so hungry for fame and fortune that he'd destroy himself to get it. That was the problem with artists. One could never tell how desperate they were until it was too late. That was why, during her stay in Annwyn, she'd renounced her muse magic.

Gathering all her hard-won restraint, she gave no more than an impersonal nod to the clerk and passed by without speaking. Perhaps he'd never be a great artist, but at least without Leanna's interference he'd have a chance for a long and happy life.

If Leanna had been full Sidhe she would have found it easier to control her muse magic. Muse magic wasn't death magic, but it had led Leanna in that direction. Full-blooded Sidhe avoided death magic, as it made them ill. Leanna, being half human, didn't possess that natural revulsion. On the contrary, she'd taken to it like a Halfling to a midsummer feast. She'd quickly become addicted to the rush. The spiral of her destruction ended with her enslavement to a depraved demon.

Now she was whole again, if still fragile. She'd taken a vow: she'd never dabble in death magic, or her muse magic, again. It was just too bad the vow didn't stop her cravings.

The elevator doors swished closed, leaving her alone in the cab. When would she grow accustomed to keeping her own company? Never, she suspected. She hated being celibate. Hated being alone. But every night since she'd escaped Hell, she'd been just that.

Her hotel room was quiet and shrouded in darkness. She didn't bother to turn on the light as she shed her dress, shoes, stockings, and bra. Wearing just her thong, she slid between the sheets. Her head sank onto a stack of downy pillows but her eyes remained open. Despite what she'd told Mac, she wasn't tired at all.

The lace curtains at the window fluttered; the hazy light from the street danced across the coverlet.

A sudden shadow fell across the bed. She blinked. She didn't at first understand what was happening.

A man's voice cut through the velvet darkness.

"*Bonsoir*, Leanna. Or at this hour, perhaps I should say *bon matin?*"

She sucked in a breath.

She wasn't alone, after all.

Chapter Three

Elflight lifted from Leanna's palm to hover over her head. The intruder was tall, with a broad chest and long, powerful legs. Death magic radiated from his body. Leanna suspected the potency she sensed was only a drop in the vast reservoir of his power. He wore a dark suit jacket over a black shirt, open at the neck. His hair, a glossy nut-brown touched by moonlight, shone. She should have been afraid, but oddly, she wasn't.

He looked familiar.

She sat up quickly, clutching the coverlet to her chest. "Do I know you?"

He smiled, a quick glint of white teeth that was anything but mirthful.

"Is your memory fading with age, Leanna? And here you promised never to forget me. But then, when you've known so many men, I suppose it's hard to keep us all straight."

He took a single step forward. Dim light bathed his features.

Leanna stared. One hand crept to her throat, her palm flattening over her pounding heart. Her lips opened, but no sound emerged.

The man snorted. "Speechless? Excuse me if I don't believe it. As I recall, you were never at a loss for words."

She swallowed. The reflex was painful. When her voice finally emerged from her throat, it was as a scratchy whisper.

"Jackson? Jackson Cabot?"

He bowed, a swift, graceful angling of the waist. So elegant. So much like the man she remembered.

But Jackson was...dead.

"You're..." She cleared her throat and began again. "You're not a ghost."

"No," he agreed.

He stepped closer, almost to the foot of the bed. Now the elflight shone full in his face, illuminating his beauty. Her mind stuttered. Jackson was human—he couldn't still be alive, not after more than a hundred years. And yet, his angled cheekbones, patrician nose, and high forehead hadn't changed at all. His hazel eyes, however, glinted with a cynical light that would have been wholly foreign to the man she'd once loved. And his complexion...that was different, too. The Jackson she'd known spent every free moment in the sun. This man's skin had nothing of Jackson's tanned, healthy glow.

Horror oozed through her veins. "You're a vampire."

"Yes." He planted both hands on the high mattress and leaned toward her. "And you, Leanna, are still a very beautiful woman."

His gaze left her face and traveled...lower.

She inched the blanket higher.

"Modest?" His tone was hard, completely lacking the teasing lilt Leanna associated with her memories of him. "I confess, I'm surprised. What are you about, returning to your hotel unaccompanied? The last thing I expected was to find you climbing into this bed alone." He straightened. "What happened to your latest conquest?"

She stared up at him, his mocking tone flowing over her as she struggled to wrap her mind around the fact that this was Jackson, *her* Jackson. Here. In her bedroom. Speaking to her. It wasn't a dream. Or a nightmare.

Then his words registered. "Conquest? What are you talking about?"

His jaw tightened. "Manannán mac Lir, the musician. I saw you with him on the television."

"You saw Mac and me on the telly?" Inane reply. Her brain refused to operate properly.

"I did. Tell me, do you screw him alone, or does the woman who was with you get in on the fun?"

Shock caused the air to puff from her lungs. "What? You think...Mac and I...and Artemis—"

"Manannán's fame has exploded in the past year. And now I find that he's traveling with you. You're a sex muse. You can't tell me your magic hasn't played a part in his—"

"Mac's success had nothing to do with my magic. For the love of all the gods in Annwyn, Jackson, Mac is my brother!"

He snorted. "Oh, really? I don't recall you ever mentioning a divine brother."

"Mac's my half-brother. We have the same mother. I never told you about him because Mac and I weren't speaking when you and I...when we were..." She lost her words. Her throat closed. Her lashes were wet.

"...in love?" Jackson prompted with more than a little sarcasm.

She met his gaze evenly. "Yes. When you and I were in love."

"Love." He spat the word. "I thought it was love, Leanna, but I soon learned how deadly your particular brand of that emotion is, didn't I?"

He paced the room. "Our affair was the definition of irony. Your other lovers wanted you for your magic; I never did. I'd been in Paris only two weeks when I realized my meager talent was nothing compared to the great masters. I'd already accepted the fact that Paris was to be just a pleasant interlude, before returning to Boston to take up the reins of my father's manufacturing empire." Turning abruptly, he faced her. "And then I found you."

"We found each other," Leanna whispered.

Jackson dragged a hand over his face. "I wanted you for my wife. I knew there was every chance you would refuse. What I didn't expect, Leanna, was that you would kill me."

The hoarse emotion in his voice sent a tremor through Leanna's body. Night after night, as that idyllic Parisian spring had unfolded, she'd lain in Jackson's arms, ear pressed to the low rumble of his chest as he told her of his life, his love, his dreams in just such fervent tones.

"But...you weren't dead when I left you! I never wanted to kill you—I just didn't want you to follow me. I made sure you had enough life essence left for a full recovery. I thought...I always assumed...you had awakened the next morning and returned to your family in Boston."

"A fine rationalization," he said. "Even for you. You knew far better than I what sort of scum roamed the alleys in Paris in those days."

Gods help her, she did.

Another ruthless glint of teeth. "Really, Leanna, you left me too soon. You should have made sure I was completely dead. Loose ends come back to strangle, sooner or later."

For the first time, she felt a glimmer of fear. "What... what happened to you that night, Jackson? I left a warding spell to protect you. No vampire could have broken it."

He crossed his arms. "No vampire except Armand Legrand."

"Oh, gods." Bile burned in the back of her throat. For a moment, she thought she would throw up.

Armand Legrand had been—and still was—the oldest and most ruthless vampire on the European continent. Depraved, cruel, and sadistic, Legrand used and discarded the lives of humans and magical creatures at whim. Even the most powerful death magic creatures gave the vampire master a wide berth.

"I provided Legrand with quite an easy meal," Jackson continued. "All my blood was intact, but because of my final interlude with you, I had very little energy left with which to flee. Legrand was so pleased with his new toy, he decided to keep me. I woke the next day, newly turned. Newly enslaved."

Leanna shuddered. The humiliation and sexual perversions the vampire master forced on his newly turned minions were known to be...

Her stomach heaved. "I'm...I'm so sorry, Jackson. So very sorry."

"You're not sorry enough, Leanna," he said softly. "At least—not yet."

Fear closed her throat. Several seconds passed before she realized the bedcovers had slipped from her numb fingers. She only noticed when Jackson's unfeeling gaze traveled to her bare breasts.

She snatched at the cotton.

"No," he said thickly. "Leave it."

She tugged the sheet higher, all the way to her chin. Her gaze flicked past him, to the door. Mac wouldn't have returned yet, but Kalen was in his room down the hall. If she screamed...

Jackson's eyes moved to her face. The raw anger evident in his expression silenced her more effectively than a gag. She didn't think she'd ever seen him angry.

The Jackson Cabot she'd once known had been a light-hearted, smiling man.

He wasn't smiling now.

"Make no mistake, Leanna. You are coming with me, and you will do as I say until I decide to let you go."

Her chin came up. "And just how do you propose to make me do that?"

He didn't answer. But his eyes changed, the brown-green irises darkening into a deep, fathomless black that seemed lit from within. Vampire mesmerism.

Leanna tried to blink to evade it. Against her will, her eyelids remained open. She tried to look away. Impossible. Gods. Jackson's mesmerism was stronger than any she'd ever encountered. How could that be? A vampire's power increased with age; only those few who had existed for many centuries could compete with Sidhe magic. Jackson had been turned only a century ago. Leanna's magic should have overcome him easily.

It didn't.

Irresistible pressure, like an invisible hand gripping her wrist, forced her arm downward. The bedcovers, clutched in her fingers, went with it. Cool cotton slithered over her chest.

She gasped a spell—Sidhe life magic, the most powerful she could muster. Her words fell dead, in a meaningless jumble of syllables. The coverlet continued its downward progress, cresting the pearled tips of her breasts, whispering across her belly. Jackson's fierce, hot gaze followed.

He controlled her movements as easily as he might have moved a puppet on a string. With his eyes, he devoured her. Her heart thumped painfully. During their time in Paris, he'd often looked at her with just that silent, intense scrutiny. Not speaking. Not touching. His mute foreplay had never failed to arouse her.

Her body remembered. Her skin heated, her heartbeat accelerated. The tips of her breasts, exposed to him now, itched. A pulling, aching sensation, like a slow fall from a high place, caught at her belly and did not let go.

She couldn't look away. His dark irises shone with vampire death magic. These were not the eyes she'd once known. Those eyes had glowed with laughter, had flashed with good humor and mischief. They'd blazed with desire, smoldered with passion. Sparked with awe and tenderness.

On one occasion—one she didn't like to remember—they'd softened with pity.

During those weeks in Paris, it had been all too easy to forget her pride and confide her deepest pain to Jackson. As soon as she had, she'd regretted it. She'd felt like a wild animal trapped in a cage. Lust she could handle. Laughter came easily. Jackson's gently sympathy and understanding—his love—had stripped her naked. It was reason she'd bolted.

The bedsheet inched past her navel. Another desperately whispered Sidhe spell failed to halt its descent. One hundred ten years ago, Jackson had been not only a talented artist, but the heir to a vast Boston family fortune. For all that, he'd only been a mundane human. He hadn't possessed even a drop of magic. And though she'd loved him, she'd always been aware that she held the upper hand.

Now he was stronger than she. She was trapped within his power. And yet she wasn't the only one chained. He was captive as well, snared by churning emotion. His sharp intake of breath, the flare of his nostrils, the clench of his jaw—all these things told of his anger. The bulge in his trousers announced his lust.

Leanna wasn't sure which emotion aroused her more.

The too-heavily spiced scent of death magic radiated from his body. If she were a proper Sidhe, she'd have been disgusted by it. Instead, it turned her on. This was Jackson, the man she'd once loved with frightening intensity. She thought he'd grown old—thought he had died. That he was standing her before her was nothing short of a miracle. She didn't care if the miracle had come wrapped in death magic. She wanted him still.

The coverlet continued its downward path, tugged by her own shaking hands. The top edge skimmed her hipbones, then snaked over her thighs. Her thong, a thin scrap of silk, was all that protected her from Jackson's consuming gaze.

His eyes flared when the sheet fell away completely. Desire twisted a sweet knife in her gut. Her belly quivered, her thighs grew slick with longing. Jackson had been a gentle lover in Paris, sweet and playful. He was no longer that gentle man. If he took her now, he'd use her roughly and slake a century of rage on the woman who had made him what he was. If he did, she wouldn't fight him, even if she could. She'd give this angry, wounded man whatever he needed.

Would he demand sex? Would he drink her blood? If he desired, he could easily drain every last drop of blood and life essence from her veins. The one thing he could not do, however, was make her like him. Sidhe could not turn vampire. Their life magic did not allow it.

Jackson's heavy footfalls rounded the foot of the bed. Fear and desire snaked through Leanna as he approached. It was perverse, humiliating, this dark wanting. She understood it too well. The yearning was very like the fatal craving she'd inspired in her artist lovers. The sins of her past had returned with a vengeance to demand their reckoning.

Jackson's shadow fell dark on her pale skin. His black gaze consumed her. She inhaled sharply. She was aware of him releasing his mesmerism. Suddenly her body was her own again. Even so, she did not move.

He smelled of fury and magic. A sheen of sweat glistened on his jaw. Strangely, the lock of brown hair that had fallen across his eyes looked softer than moonlight. She longed to reach up and stroke it.

She didn't dare.

She lay tense, waiting for his move. Excruciating moments passed.

He didn't touch her.

And yet he didn't move away.

She wet her lips with her tongue. "What...what is it you want from me, Jackson? Revenge?"

He seemed not to hear. He reached out, as if he meant to touch her. Her belly clenched, dreading and craving the contact.

His hand dropped to his side and curled into a fist.

"You look just the same," he said at last, more to himself than to her. "How is that possible? Sidhe age slowly, but not that slowly. Not when half their essence is human."

"I spent a year in Annwyn. The magic of the Otherworld...it restored my youth."

Surprise flickered in his eyes. "Annwyn? You told me once you weren't welcome there. That your Sidhe mother refused to acknowledge you."

Her cheeks flamed. He knew too much. He knew her mother, Queen of Annwyn, had abandoned her half-human daughter. He knew Leanna's human father had been a drunken brute who hadn't been able to control his carnal urges when his pubescent daughter's Sidhe sex magic had first made itself known. She had whispered those humiliating confessions to Jackson in the darkness one night. His pity had made her burn with shame.

She knew he remembered. His eyes were far too knowing. She wanted to look away, but he didn't allow it. He held her pinned, body and soul, like a live butterfly on a naturalist's board.

"That's not quite true anymore," she said.

"Explain."

"I practiced death magic." In a way, it was a relief to talk about it. "I thought I could control it. I learned that I couldn't. A demon took me captive and dragged me to the death realms. I was trapped there for a year, until Mac—my brother—found me. He got me out, and then convinced our mother to allow me into Annwyn. I was...old and haggard. I needed healing."

"And now you're young again. Beautiful and deadly. Free to beguile. Free to kill."

"No! Not anymore. I—"

He leaned over her, his face scant inches away. His right hand came down over her mouth, smothering her words.

"Silence. Lie still."

She sensed him waging some inner battle. After several tense moments, a rush of breath left his lips. His shoulders collapsed a fraction. It seemed like he'd accepted a defeat of some kind, but exactly what had conquered him she couldn't imagine. Jackson clearly was the one holding all the power in this encounter.

His right hand still covered her mouth. Now his left hand touched her—first one breast, then the other. Had she expected harshness? His handling of her wasn't abrupt or angry at all. He stroked her with consummate delicacy. She was reminded of the afternoon she'd come to his studio overlooking the Seine. His soft-bristled brush had swept over her breasts in just the same way.

On that long-ago morning, Jackson's lovemaking had left her languid and sated. And yet, she'd been assaulted by nagging doubts. Calling it a test of sorts, she'd released just a small taste of her muse magic. She hoped he'd resist it—she hoped his love for her was greater than his ambition.

He had accepted it, eagerly. She'd watched, a curious numbness spreading through her, as he leaped from the bed and anointed his brush with paint. He stroked her image onto canvas with sure, swift strokes. The portrait had been, of course, a masterpiece.

Now, in this dead crypt so far from the lights of Paris and the disillusions of her first—and only—true love, Leanna's body became Jackson's canvas. His fingertips brushed her nipples...stroked her belly...circled her navel. He drew a line downward, sketching the rise and fall of her Venus mound. He paused—too delicately—at the place that throbbed for him.

Her thighs parted—whether at his silent command or in response to her own yearning, she didn't know. His fingers explored between her legs, stroking either side of the damp fabric of her thong. She moaned and arched shamelessly, offering herself to his hand.

He watched her closely as he touched her. She blinked up at him, and fear rushed to do battle with her lust. His expression had darkened. His brows were drawn, and his eyes burned. His hand, still clamped over her mouth, flexed. A cold knot of fear formed in Leanna's belly and tightened.

Slowly he lifted his hands from her lips and body. He placed both palms on her pillow, one on each side of her head. His breath rasped; her chest heaved.

Their gazes clashed. A metallic scent—like death, like blood wrapped her like a noose. Her body responded; she couldn't help it. She'd been a practitioner of death magic. She'd endured a year as a demonwhore in the death realms. It didn't matter that she'd finally been welcomed in Annwyn, didn't matter that she'd dedicated herself to light and life magic.

Leanna may have forsworn death magic, but in a deep, denied part of her soul, she still longed for it. Her memory of the death magic highs she'd experienced could never be erased. She was sure that sex with Jackson—as he was now—would blow her mind.

He lowered himself to the bed. His long, powerful body stretched out along her right side, his torso supported on his elbow. The mattress dipped under his weight, causing her to roll toward him, until every part of her softening body pressed against hard, unyielding muscle.

She felt his erection thickening against her belly. "Jackson—"

"Silence."

He captured her chin in his fingers, peering intently into her eyes. She lay still, silent as he'd commanded. Chaotic sensations racked her body. She wet her lips, and his eyes darkened dangerously.

"Temptress," he whispered. "Siren."

The words dropped like pebbles into a taut pool of anticipation. Ripples radiated to every corner of her soul. Jackson's body trembled almost as violently as her own.

"No." His voice shook. "I will not allow you to destroy me once again."

"I would never do that. I—"

"Silence!"

All protest died in her throat. She waited for him to act, her heart pounding against her ribs. For several long moments, he didn't move, leaving Leanna to wonder what held him back.

And then nothing held him back.

Chapter Four

Jackson, in his vast pride, had believed his control unshakable.

To his eternal humiliation he found that it was not. His resolve slipped and tumbled down a long slope to ruin. His kiss, meant to be brutal, became as soft as a prayer.

Leanna's lips were soft and tasted faintly of cherries.

Taste begat scent; scent begat sensation and images. Memories assaulted his brain. He recalled the evening he'd first set eyes on her, at a party given by a mutual friend. Her red hair shone in candlelight, her pointed ears delicate and impossibly erotic. She'd seemed so fragile, and somehow inexpressibly sad.

His fingers had brushed hers when he'd presented her with a flute of champagne. He'd asked her to dance. She'd refused. Her faint Scots accent had intrigued him.

He'd asked her a second time. And a third.

Finally, he'd made her laugh, and she'd accepted.

Their first dance was a waltz. Afterward, they'd strolled through their host's garden. From then on, they were inseparable. They'd wandered the streets of Montmartre, joined the crowds at the Moulin Rouge.

They'd ascended Gustave Eiffel's new folly, and marveled at Paris laid out at their feet.

In the darkest hours of the early morning, they'd made love...

His palm grazed her breast, riding on memories. Fingers tightened on soft flesh. His kiss turned urgent. This was dangerous, he knew. He was falling again—too far, too fast. If he didn't pull away in time...

He needed to remember why he'd come to her. Not for this. He'd meant for her to become the tool of his triumph, not of his destruction.

He gathered his resolve. He almost put his good sense into motion. But then Leanna whimpered against his mouth and arched into his hand, her nipple pebbling in his palm. And he realized the helpless sound she made was not fear, but desire.

Lust shot through him like lightning. The magic that kept his heart beating—death magic—reared its ugly head. Hunger, sexual hunger, too long repressed, battered his defenses. His tongue invaded her mouth; his fangs erupted. Shuddering, he fought the urge to bite hard and deep. The sheer effort blanked his mind.

She should have been fighting him. She wasn't. Just the opposite—her arms stole around him, stroking, kneading, entwining about his neck. Her legs wrapped around his hips. He shook with the strength of his need. It had been more than seven decades since he'd had a woman. Too long, by any man's reckoning.

She licked his ear. Her legs squeezed his torso. Magic—life magic—broke over him. It was like a bucket of ice thrown on a raging fire.

Abruptly his sanity snapped into place. What the hell was he doing?

He tore his lips from hers. He grabbed her calves and wrenched her legs from around his waist. He thrust himself off her body to stand at her bedside, staring down at her beauty, his chest heaving painfully. She gazed up at him, flushed and panting. Bewildered but willing. Very willing.

God help him. He closed his eyes, clenched his fists, and concentrated on his most complicated mantra.

"Jackson—" Her voice was no more than a whisper of breath.

He opened his eyes and immediately regretted it. She was so beautiful Gazing on her dislodged something deep in his chest, in the vicinity of his dead heart. Her long auburn hair spilled in glossy abundance all around—just as it had in Paris. Her face was perfection. And her eyes... Ah, her wide gray eyes held the same hint of sadness that had once drawn him so profoundly to her side. Her thick lashes were wet with her tears.

She was trembling.

And so was he.

He repressed a rush of sympathy, replacing it with anger. He'd seen Leanna's tears. Seen her use them as weapons. A sharpened sword couldn't cut a man to shreds with more efficiency than the feminine grief she manufactured so easily. She'd cried that last night in Paris, too. Scant moments later, she offered him the full force of her muse magic and tricked him into releasing almost all his life essence.

If he wasn't careful, she would lure him to ruin again.

She reached for him. "Jackson? What's wrong?"

"You will find," he said tersely, "that I am no longer the fool I once was."

"You were never a fool, Jackson."

He grabbed for the bedpost, steadying himself. "Get dressed. Your body no longer interests me."

He ignored the flash of hurt in her eyes. Turning, he paced to the window, where he looked to the street below, seeing nothing but the scenes flashing through his own mind. The bed creaked; Leanna's footsteps padded across the carpet. A drawer opened. He heard the whisper of fabric on skin.

Her silent obedience brought him a measure of satisfaction. He imagined her on her knees, obeying him in other ways, her rosy, pouting lips opening...

God*damn* it. He shut his eyes, called his mantra, willed his raging erection to wilt. Slowly, it did. He sensed Leanna behind him, watching. Calmer now, but not yet ready to face her, he opened his eyes and peered once more through the glass. A lone figure paced the cobblestones. Gunter. He sensed Enzo and Solange nearby as well.

He willed his minion to glance up at the window. Gunter's gaze lifted immediately. A flick of his Jackson's fingers, a thought directed to the young vampire's mind, was all that was needed to communicate his orders.

Gunter nodded and moved out of sight.

Jackson turned to face Leanna. He would not allow her to distract him from his purpose. She had destroyed his past. It was only fitting that he use her to ensure his future.

He didn't immediately speak. Instead, he watched her grow increasingly uncertain in the face of his silence. She'd donned a simple knit dress. Off-white. Clinging. The hem fell demurely to her knees. Her unbound breasts looked even more tantalizing covered than they had bare.

She'd stepped into low-heeled sandals. Her fingers twisted together and her pulse skittered. Her face was very pale.

"What are you going to do with me?"

He told her the truth. "Use you."

Her gray eyes widened. "How? For what?"

"You'll find out soon enough."

"And if I don't agree?"

He laughed, harshly. "I'm afraid you have no choice. This time around, mine is the greater power. I can make you dance like a marionette."

He lifted a hand, fingers spread, and captured her gaze. He unleashed a small tendril of his vampire mesmerism and allowed his power to strike.

Leanna's body jerked.

He willed her to walk across the room.

Her limbs responded. She tried to resist his command, but her efforts were fruitless. He toyed with her, relaxing his will and letting her believe she'd broken his control, then swiftly overpowering her again. Finally, he allowed her to sink to her knees.

Illicit fantasies exploded in his brain. With a curse, he jerked her back to her feet, more roughly than he'd intended. At her gasp of pain, his self-hatred burned more fiercely than it ever had.

"Jackson, please. Don't. Don't do this. I'll come with you willingly. Only...tell me why." She drew a breath. "Do you mean to kill me?"

"No." Dear God, he knew now he could never do it.

"What, then? Please, tell me—"

She broke off as the bedroom door swung open. Gunter entered, Enzo on his heels. Solange crossed the threshold last and closed the door behind her. Leanna's gaze flew to the other woman. For several seconds, the two females stood motionless, assessing each other.

Enzo and Gunter looked at him expectantly.

"Take her," Jackson told them.

***

Leanna's eyes opened on stygian darkness. Groggy and disoriented, she struggled to marshal her thoughts. The edges of her mind fuzzed for a long time before she finally succeeded.

She had no idea where Jackson might have taken her. She remembered only fragments of the journey, and none too clearly, though she had been conscious for it. Vampire magic. The undead regularly toyed with the minds of the living.

Leanna had known many vampires in her long life. Thankfully, the vampire master Armand Legrand had not been one of them. Whenever she'd been in Paris, she'd scrupulously avoided meeting him. It hadn't been too difficult; Legrand preferred to dwell underground.

She lay on a soft surface—a bed, perhaps. Her clothing was intact. She sniffed the air. Damp. Musty. The flat smell of ancient death lingered. She tried, unsuccessfully, to suppress a shiver.

Fighting the haze in her mind, she searched for her magic. The power was there, but far away, behind a thick curtain of death magic. Touching the light was like stretching her arm across a chasm. The flicker of elflight she managed to call was very weak.

The illumination spread just below a rocky ceiling. Shadows resolved into shapes. Her prison seemed to be a narrow cave. A silk carpet hugged the ground; brocaded fabric draped the walls. The edges of the wall-hangings touched bare rock. About fifteen feet from the foot of the bed, a tapestry hung the width of the space shielding the makeshift room from whatever lay beyond.

Furnishings were sparse but elegant. A table, two straight-backed chairs, an iron stand bearing unlit candles, a deep leather armchair. With a start, Leanna realized the latter was occupied by the somber young woman Jackson had admitted to Leanna's hotel room. Leanna eyed her curiously.

She spoke. "Ah, so you are awake. At last."

She was lovely, with dark, curling hair. She spoke English with a French accent. Rising with catlike grace, she clasped her hands and inclined her head in Leanna's direction as if they'd just been introduced at a party. Leanna scrutinized her aura. She was human. Powerful. Alive, not vampire. A death witch.

She rose and lit a brace of candles on an iron stand. As the flames leapt to life, Leanna let her elflight die.

"Who are you?" she asked. "Where is Jackson?"

"The master commanded me to watch over you," the witch said.

"You are...?"

"The master's steward, of course."

The explanation caused Leanna to tense. Vampires required magical human stewards to safeguard their sleeping places and perform various daylight tasks. Death witches were especially prized for the role. Most vampires also used their stewards sexually, but this woman was so young. Barely out of her teens, Leanna guessed. Surely Jackson wasn't physically intimate with her. Then again, what did she really know of the man Jackson had become?

As if called from her thoughts, Jackson's voice intruded. "Solange. You may leave us now."

Immediately, the girl turned and bowed. "Oui, monsieur." She rounded the edge of the tapestry and disappeared.

Jackson stepped into the candlelight. Leanna studied him. His features were stark, his skin very pale. The expression in his eyes was completely devoid of emotion. It chilled her to the bone.

A tear trickled down her cheek. She'd turned him into this dark, dead creature. Of all the many sins she'd committed in her life, what she'd done to Jackson was perhaps the worst, because he'd loved her so well. Perhaps as much as he hated her now.

"Crying, Leanna?" His tone mocked. "You? You surprise me."

She blinked and was shocked to find him suddenly very close, leaning over her bed. His dark gaze raked her body. He'd crossed the room so quickly and silently she hadn't perceived his motion at all.

She swallowed the lump in her throat and wished she could stop her tears.

"That young witch. Is she your lover?" She despised herself for caring, and for asking.

He stiffened and drew back. "No. She is merely my steward."

"She's very young for a steward."

She thought he would give a curt reply to that, if he replied at all. To her surprise, he didn't.

"That would be true for most witches, but not Solange. She is exceptionally talented. Her grandfather was a powerful sorcerer who served as my steward for nearly fifty years. He began her magical training even before she could talk. Three years ago, upon his death, she assumed his role."

"Three years! How old was she then?"

"Sixteen."

"And you allowed it?"

His lips twisted. "I had little choice. She refused to leave me. Jean-Claude joined us soon after, in any case."

"Jean-Claude?"

He seemed to come back to himself, as if he'd only now remembered he was speaking to a woman he hated. "Jean-Claude was a young death sorcerer Solange and I encountered in Marseilles. He became my second steward and soon after, he and Solange married." His voice hardened. "Three months ago, he was taken by Legrand."

"Killed?"

"I do not know."

His tone was grim, and with good reason. If Jean-Claude was not known to be dead, there was a good chance he'd been turned and enslaved by Legrand or one of his minions. Many would choose death to that fate.

Jackson was no doubt contemplating the same truth. His expression darkened dangerously. Leanna cast about for another topic.

"What is this place, Jackson? Are we underground?"

"Yes. My minions stand guard. No one's coming to rescue you, Leanna, if that's what you're hoping."

He turned and lifted the velvet wall hanging nearest the bed. Deep shelves pierced the cave wall, each just long and deep enough to support a human body. In fact, several berths did contain mummified skeletons, wrapped in rotting linen.

"This is a crypt," she said.

"Yes. An undiscovered tributary of the Catacombs of St. Domitilla, to be precise."

He let the velvet fall. "Just think, Leanna. Above our heads living humans go about their daily tasks, blessedly ignorant of the abomination of death lurking beneath the rock they trod. Up there, life essence and life magic abound. For them the sky is blue. For them the sun shines." He exhaled. "The sun. I have not seen it for more than one hundred years. I live in darkness, Leanna."

"Because of me." A tear dripped across her cheek. "I'm sorry for that, Jackson. More than you know." She fought to remain calm. "Why did you bring me here? Is it revenge you're after?"

He didn't immediately answer. His heated gaze was bold on her body, lingering on her breasts and the vee between her thighs. She drew up her knees and wrapped her arms around them.

"Modesty, Leanna? I did not think the word was in your vocabulary."

"I won't fight you, if that's what you think. I know you're the wronged party here."

Shadows draped his lower body; she couldn't tell whether or not he was aroused. Gods help her, she was. Dark longing twisted in her belly Moisture flooded her thighs. Jackson's nostrils flared; his eyes narrowed. She was sure he sensed how soft and ready she was for whatever he chose to do. And yet he made no move.

"You would like me to climb into that bed, wouldn't you? So you can siphon off the stolen life essence that allows me this poor imitation of life?"

"No, Jackson, you're wrong. I would never use my sex magic against you."

He gave a bitter laughed. "You'll forgive me if I don't believe you. You call yourself a creature of life magic, but you thrive on death. You're a perversion of nature."

She shuddered. His assessment was as accurate as an arrow to the heart. How many nights had she lain awake in Annwyn, fearing exactly that: her magic was flawed, an aberration of death amid life.

"What do you want of me, Jackson?"

"As it happens, I do want your magic, Leanna. I want the worst of it."

"You want to die?"

"No. Perhaps it's true that I would be better off dead, but it would be impossible for me to pursue that end. A vampire's instinct for survival is too great. No, it's not my own existence I wish to obliterate with your magic, but another's."

She inhaled sharply. "You want me to murder someone for you?"

His lips drew back, baring even white teeth. She saw no hint of fangs. "Yes. A simple task, to drain the life essence from a lover. After all, you've done it often, and thoroughly, in the past. You will do it again for me. Once my enemy is destroyed, I'll release you unharmed."

"No, Jackson." Her voice trembled. "I can't do it. I...I've renounced my muse magic. I won't use it to kill anyone, not ever again. Not even for you."

"You'll do as I command." He leaned forward, his pose deceptively casual. "If not willingly, then under my compulsion. You have no choice."

She looked into his eyes and knew he spoke the truth. He could—and would—force her to his will. "Please understand. In Annwyn, I swore an oath that I would never kill again."

"A pity, then, that you'll have to break your vow."

"No. I won't." She swallowed. "I'd do almost anything to atone for the suffering I've caused you, but I won't kill for you. You may be stronger than me, but my brother is vastly more powerful than you. Mac can easily put a stop to this crazy scheme. As soon as he realizes I'm missing—"

"He'll find the message you left on his voice mail. You've told him not to worry. You've decided a few days at a spa in Tuscany will do you a world of good." He mocked her surprise. "What? You've forgotten? How strange."

"That ruse won't work for long."

"I won't need your services for long," he replied. "Tonight is all I require. This evening, you'll pay a visit to my enemy's vampire club and engage in a bit of lethal sex play."

"You want me to kill another vampire?"

He inclined his head.

She experienced a twinge of foreboding. Surely Jackson was strong enough to defeat almost any vampire he might encounter. Except...

"Who?" she asked.

"Why, Armand Legrand, of course."

Chapter Five

"Armand Legrand! Why—you can't possibly be serious!"

Leanna's eyes were wide, gray, and utterly horrified. She swallowed. Jackson watched her throat flex. The flutter of her pulse—just *there,* beneath her sweet, tender skin—tormented him. Unbidden, his fangs erupted, the points scraping the inside of his mouth. Damn it all to hell. He'd fed only scant hours before, but now burning thirst scraped his throat raw. He hadn't thirsted for a woman so fiercely in the seventy long years of his self-imposed celibacy. He was as ravenous as if he'd gone without blood for months.

It would be so easy to drink from her. To nip the rapid pulses at her neck, her wrist, her groin. She would taste like sunshine. And Jackson had been living in darkness for so very long.

Could he allow himself the indulgence? One small sip? Taking Leanna's blood wouldn't dim his own power. Just the opposite—her Sidhe blood, so potent with life essence, would strengthen him. The danger lay in the near-certainty that the bite would lead to more. To physical carnality. Plunging his cock into Leanna's ripe body, breaking his long-held vows, would drain his power. And if she offered her muse magic, he very much feared he would squander seventy years' worth of hoarded life essence in a blink of an eye—all for the chance of becoming, for a few scant moments, the artist and lover he'd once been.

He was heavy with need, the blood pulsing slow and hard in his loins. Leanna rubbed her bare arms, causing the knit fabric of her dress to stretch across her breasts. His eyes followed the movement. His groin tightened. It was far too arousing having her here in his lair. In his bed. He could not let himself forget how very dangerous she was.

She was afraid of him, as he had intended her to be. Part of him—the part that clung to his humanity—hated her fear, hated that he had caused it. The man he'd once been would never have tormented a woman this way. Especially this woman. Once, he'd wanted nothing more than to hold her in his arms and protect her from the sadness that only he seemed to see in her eyes. Perhaps her vulnerability had been nothing but an illusion. But no. When he looked at her now, he saw that the sadness still remained, and he didn't doubt it was real. To his shame, he still wanted to banish it.

He was a fool.

He dared not do so much as lay a finger on her. Because even after all the time that had passed, even after what her betrayal had cost him, he still burned for her. If he touched her, it would not stop at that. Decades of waiting, of plotting his vengeance on Legrand, would go up in flames.

With a power born of long, agonizing practice, he battered his sexual hunger into submission. Only when he'd brought his appetite under some semblance of control did he allow himself to look at her.

"I assure you," he said, "I am deadly serious."

"I don't understand. How could I possibly kill such a powerful vampire? He could crush me in an instant."

"I don't believe that's true. Legrand was once, long ago during his human life, a brilliant artist. I believe your muse magic will affect him greatly."

"You can't be serious. Legrand is an artist?"

"Was. He is no longer, of course. Being vampire tends to exert a negative influence on one's creativity. We are much more comfortable dealing with death and decay. But the longing remains." He paused. "I know that as well as any."

"But...how did you discover Legrand's past? Did he speak of it?"

"No, never. But he has an unfinished illuminated manuscript is in his possession, a medieval relic of which he is exceedingly protective. It's a hand-inscribed copy of the New Testament of the Bible, completed as far as First Galatians.

"That's an odd artifact for a vampire to own," Leanna said.

"Indeed," Jackson agreed. "He keeps it locked away; I imagine few of his minions even know of its existence. He kept me very close for the twenty-five years before my escape, however. Often, I was his only...companion...for nights on end. On some of those nights, he retrieved the manuscript from its hiding place and pored over it, page by page, for hours." The exercise invariably left him in the darkest of moods. Which he would turn on his favorite slave.

"You believe Legrand was the artist who created this manuscript?"

"I do. After I escaped, I made it my business to discover everything about my former master. It took years of digging, but eventually I learned Legrand, when living, had been a French monk. He spent decades laboring over an exquisite illuminated New Testament. He'd not yet finished the Epistles of St. Paul when his monastery was overrun by a horde of rampaging vampires. All the monks were either killed or turned. Legrand became the leader of the survivors. His band of vampire monks quickly became the scourge of the surrounding countryside."

Leanna licked dry lips. "You want me to...to have sex with Legrand, and tempt him with my muse magic? And then...try to kill him?"

"Not try. I want you to do it. Don't think of it as killing, if that eases your conscience. Legrand is vampire. He's already dead."

"You want me to end his existence. It amounts to the same thing."

"Once he's dust, I'll set you free."

"Please Jackson, just let me go. Nothing good can come of this."

He averted his eyes. "You won't be alone when you go to him, if that's what you fear. My minions will protect you." He paused and looked back at her. "I will protect you."

"But...your plan is insane. Even if I did approach Legrand—you forget that Legrand and I both lived in Paris for decades. We never met face-to-face—I wasn't so foolish in those days as to confront him. But even though I avoided crossing paths with him, I know he tracked every magical being who entered his territory. He certainly knows of me and my muse magic. He'd never willingly take me to his bed."

"He has little reason to expect a Sidhe would come calling at his door. You won't have any trouble slipping past his minions. Cast a glamour. He'll see you as just another vampire addict looking for a blood high. He won't realize who you are until it's too late for him to resist your magic."

Her lashes swept downward. "I can't do it, Jackson. I can't break the vows I made in Annwyn. Don't you understand? I swore on Annwyn's tree of life! I swore on my soul!"

"And what of my soul, Leanna? The one you've doomed to an eternity of waking death?"

"I wronged you, I know. I'm so sorry for that. If there was any way to undo what I did that night...I'd give my life to change the past. But please, don't ask me to do this."

Jackson hesitated, his jaw clenched so tightly that pain spiked into his ear. His first instinct was to pardon her for her crimes, and release her from his control—no matter that she was the one who'd condemned him to his dark, depraved existence. He summoned the image of Legrand's face, twisted in perverted pleasure and found the courage to go on.

"I'm not asking you to do it, Leanna. I am commanding you."

"Do you really have that much power, Jackson? I think you're conning me. You can compel me to have sex with Legrand—I don't doubt that. But can you really force me to use my Sidhe magic against him? You're powerful, yes, but are you that powerful?"

"I am."

Her plea took on an edge of desperation. "What makes you think my muse magic is strong enough to drain a vampire as powerful as Legrand? He's hoarding almost a millennia of life essence! I'll never be able to drain him completely."

"Then that is the solution to your moral dilemma," Jackson said evenly. "You needn't kill Legrand. Weaken him and I will gladly finish him off." He placed his palms on the edge of the bed and leaned toward her. "You owe me that, at least, Leanna."

He was all too aware a note of supplication had crept into his voice. He hated that almost as much as he hated the thought of Leanna giving her body to Legrand. But God help him, with her magic on his side, it could all be over tonight. Legrand could be dust before the next dawn. He was willing to sacrifice anything for that.

Scant inches separated his lips from her skin. He could hear her Sidhe blood, so strong, so sweet, so alive, pulsing through her veins. He wanted it. He wanted her.

She regarded him with shadowed eyes. Slowly, she unfolded her body from its defensive pose. When she rose on her knees and reached for him, placing one delicate hand on his forearm, he flinched.

"I can...imagine...what you suffered at Legrand's hands. And now you want vengeance. I understand the desire for vengeance, Jackson, more than you know. But revenge won't make you whole. It would be better just to walk away. You escaped Legrand's influence years ago— why have you stayed in his territory all this time? Why not go home, to Boston? Why not forget Legrand and make a new life?"

"Run like a beaten dog? I think not."

"Don't think of it as defeat. Think of it as the start of a new life. You could come with me to Scotland. Legrand's influence doesn't reach into the Highlands. You'd be content there."

Content? In a world that included Legrand? It was not possible. The vampire master had burned his putrid essence into the marrow of Jackson's soul. The pain, the humiliation, the insanity of being slave to that monster would never fade. The horror of Jackson's first kill, the shame he felt in draining and using the victims Legrand had chosen, the sexual perversions he'd been forced to visit on innocents—and those Legrand had forced on Jackson—those rancid memories would never leave him. He was tainted, dirty. Sometimes his rage at what he'd endured, what he'd become, was so profound he wondered how his body could contain it. He would never be clean, never have peace. But he could, at least, have the satisfaction of seeing Legrand turned to dust.

And then there was Jean-Claude's fate to consider. Jackson could not have loved a son of his own flesh more. Legrand's minions had taken Solange's husband. Had they killed him? Or was Jean-Claude even now suffering the same horrors Jackson had endured as a newly turned vampire? Jackson couldn't rest until he knew.

"I vowed to destroy Legrand," he said quietly. "I will use any weapon at my disposal. Especially you, Leanna."

***

Jackson was gone before a protest could form on Leanna's lips. The heavy tapestry barely stirred in the wake of his passing. Leanna remained motionless for a long moment, resisting the urge to follow. Best to let some time pass. Mac was no fool. Since Leanna had emerged from Annwyn with her newfound determination to embrace only the light, he'd kept a brotherly eye on her, ready to come to her assistance should she need him. He'd figure out soon enough that she wasn't lolling about at a Tuscan spa. If she could put off Jackson's mad scheme until Mac found her, she was sure she could...

What? Convince Mac to help one vampire kill another? That scheme was even more ludicrous than Jackson's. A Sidhe demigod wasn't likely to come to the aid of a vampire. He was more likely to hope the participants in a feud did away with each other.

Well. She'd just have to convince her brother that Jackson was worth saving.

Restless, she climbed off the bed and made a circuit of the room. The tapestries were very fine, but the thought of the dead humans lying behind them made her shiver. The twin mahogany chairs bore the patina of age, the backs imaginatively carved with scenes of a boar hunt. The table between them was polished so brightly, she could see her reflection in the dark mirror of its surface. A leather-bound book, lay open upon it. Machiavelli's *Il Principe*.

She edged toward the tapestry that shielded the chamber's exit. She'd almost resolved to explore behind it when the heavy fabric stirred. Jackson's young steward emerged from the darkness beyond, followed by a tall vampire minion.

Solange stood aside as the vampire deposited a red leather suitcase on the floor, then, nodding to the steward, left the room. The bag was Leanna's own.

"Enzo took the liberty of packing your things while I checked you out of your hotel." Solange surveyed Leanna, her dislike evident in the coolness of her expression. Her smooth dark hair, cut short, caught the glimmer of the candles. "It would have seemed odd for you to leave your things behind."

Of course. It would have been little trouble for the witch, with the aid of vampire mesmerism, to present the illusion of Leanna voluntarily leaving the hotel. "I'm surprised you didn't toss the lot into the nearest rubbish bin," she said.

"I was tempted," Solange replied. "But the master ordered it be brought to you. You do not possess, however, appropriate attire for a vampire club. I have purchased what you need for your visit to Legrand's lair. You will find it in your bag."

Leanna eyed her. "You don't seem enthralled by the idea."

Her lashes swept downward. "It is not my place to question the master's decisions."

"Perhaps not, but you do anyway."

Solange's lips firmed. "If I question anything, it is his association with one such as you. I know who you are. Your reappearance in his life bodes ill. You nearly killed him once. This time, I fear you will succeed."

"You're wrong," Leanna said quietly. "The last thing I want to do is hurt Jackson."

"What one wants, and what one does, are often two separate things." Solange twisted a gold band on the fourth finger of her left hand. A wedding ring, Leanna realized.

"It would have been better had you never come to Rome. The master has been patient for years. Now, so close to the endgame, he grows dangerously restless. Encountering you has only encouraged his folly. He will advance when he should wait."

"If you believe that, then help me get out of here."

"I will not disobey the master's orders."

"Not even to save him?"

Solange shook her head. "I will not break my vows. If necessary, I will follow him into death."

"That's rubbish."

"No." Jackson appeared at the edge of the tapestry. "That is loyalty. Something that you, Leanna, know nothing about." He eyed his steward's bowed head. "You may leave us, my dear."

She nodded and was gone.

He advanced toward Leanna. Unconsciously, she took a step back. He smiled.

"Afraid of me?"

"No," she said.

"Then you're a fool."

"That's more than likely."

"Lie on the bed, Leanna."

"What?" Her brief hesitation was met with a flare of dark light in his eyes and a tugging sensation in her limbs, reminding her of his power to compel her obedience. Rather than humiliate herself with resistance, she obeyed. Climbing onto the mattress, she lay on her back, watching him.

"Dawn is not far off," he said. "It's too late to confront Legrand tonight. This evening when I wake...then we will act."

"We?" she asked.

"I will remain close. To ensure your compliance."

"Jackson, let's talk about this. I—" She broke off when he suddenly appeared at her side. He snared her wrist. Her eyes widened as she noted two lengths of chain dangled from his hand. Before she quite knew what had happened, he'd closed a padded leather manacle around her wrist. She watched, aghast, as he fastened the steel cuff attached to the other end around the iron bed post.

She twisted her wrist, trying to wriggle her hand free, but the cuff was far too tight and laced with a dark spell. A wave of panic ensued. She was all too familiar with death magic fetters and the horrors that visited those bound by them.

"Jackson, no! What do you think you're doing?"

He caught her flailing free arm and secured it with a second cuff. "I told you, dawn is not far off. With the coming of the sun, a vampire sleeps. While Solange and my minions are strong, I am not at all sure that their magic is up to the task of preventing your escape. So I am taking precautions."

"Let me go." She shut her eyes, and tried to stop her body from trembling. "I won't try to escape. You have my word."

"I'm afraid that isn't quite sufficient." He turned to leave.

"No!" She hated the note of panic in her voice, but was unable to stop it. The death magic sinking into her flesh made rational thought impossible.

He turned back to her, frowning as he noted her body's tremors.

"Please," she begged. "You don't understand. You can't leave me like this. I—"

"Master!" A corner of the tapestry was wrenched aside, revealing Gunter, half doubled over, his hands on his thigh, trying to catch his breath. Solange hovered behind him.

Jackson took two swift steps toward them. "What? What is it?"

"On the surface," Gunter panted. "Jean-Claude. Enzo has seen him. As we feared, he is vampire. And he is..." He fell silent as his eyes darted toward Solange.

The witch swayed dangerously on her feet. Jackson was beside her in an instant, one arm encircling her back as he led her to a chair. She sank down to sit with her head bowed. Jackson's gaze met Gunter's over her head.

"Go on," he said evenly.

The young vampire gave a slight nod. "Jean-Claude is on a blood rampage." Leanna fought a surge of revulsion. Newly made vampires were ravenous, but their ability to control their unfamiliar magic was negligible. The blood rampage of such a creature was truly horrendous.

"How bad?" asked Jackson.

"There is a trail of blood upon the city cobblestones, connecting at least a half dozen dead bodies."

"Who is his handler?" Jackson demanded. "Surely not Legrand himself. He rarely appears on the surface."

"No, monsieur. It is Xaviere."

Jackson let out a low curse. "That bastard is almost as depraved as his master."

Solange raised her head. Her eyes were haunted. "Jackson. We must—"

"Of course we must. There is no question."

Swiftly, he stood. "Stay here," he told the girl. "Gunter and I will join Enzo on the surface. Xaviere is a mere deputy. I am more than a match for him."

"But I—" Solange began.

Jackson was already ducking past the edge of the tapestry, Gunter on his heels. The pair disappeared into the dark tunnel beyond. Solange rose shakily to her feet, one hand gripping the back of her chair. After a brief hesitation, she straightened and set out after them.

"Wait!" Leanna cried. She twisted, pulling at the chains that bound her arms. "Solange, wait! Please!"

The witch hesitated, turning, a death grip on the edge of the tapestry.

"Jean-Claude is your husband."

Surprise flickered in her eyes. "Yes. He was taken by Legrand. We did not know for certain what had happened—" She faltered, then turned. "I must go—"

"No! Wait! Will...will Jackson and his minions be able to free him from his handler?"

Solange's grip on the tapestry tightened. "I do not know. Xaviere is very strong, but certainly my master is stronger. But even if he succeeds, he will be weakened by the fight. Legrand is sly and his spies have been tracking Monsieur Cabot for decades. I fear he has set Jean-Claude on rampage so close to our hiding place precisely to draw him out." Again, she turned away. "I cannot stay here. The master will need my magic."

"I can help, too," Leanna said urgently. "Are you able to unlock these manacles?"

"Of course."

"Then do it. Release me and my magic is yours."

"I have no reason to trust you." Solange's eyes flicked to the chains above Leanna's head. "And neither, it appears, does my master."

With that, she ducked behind the tapestry and disappeared.

"Wait—" Leanna pleaded with an empty room. She twisted her wrists fruitlessly in the manacles, her panic growing with each ragged breath. Her magic felt so far away. Each time she grasped for it, nothing was there. Death magic wrapped her in its tempting, suffocating grip. She was a fish on the shore, gasping through useless gills.

She couldn't stay trussed like this for long, she'd go mad! If the unthinkable happened and Jackson and his minions lost their battle...

Time passed, measured only by her ragged breath and the rapid melt of candle wax. She tried not to dwell on the horror of what might be happening above ground. Eyes fixed on the light, she watched as the flames, one by one, sputtered and died.

When a gust of hot air swept down the tunnel, stirring the edges of the tapestry and extinguishing the last guttering candle, she was left alone in the dark with nothing but fear.

Chapter Six

Even though Jackson knew full well what to expect, his first sight of Jean-Claude hit him with all the force of a fist to the gut.

"There," whispered Enzo, pointing. "In the doorway."

Dawn was less than an hour away. From his vantage point on the rooftop, with eyes well accustomed to darkness, Jackson had no trouble making out the grisly scene below. A wet slick defining the vampire's path gave the alley the appearance of a twisting river of blood. A mangled corpse, limbs sickly askew, lay on the cobblestones. Jean-Claude crouched beside the huddled figure.

He was very glad Solange was safely underground.

Jackson knew well enough that Jean-Claude had had no choice in what he'd done this night. A new vampire was a deadly creature in the best of circumstances, when handled by a responsible master. When controlled by such depraved and perverted creatures as Legrand and Xaviere, however...

Memories of Jackson's own first rampage battered his brain. His path of carnage had been as grisly, if not more so, than Jean-Claude's. He'd woken the next night, sated in body and sick in soul. Years had passed before he faced the guilt of his first night of killing.

The nights that had come after had been easier. Which was, perhaps, an even greater horror.

"He won't rest for long," Gunter muttered. "With the amount of blood he must have taken tonight, I'm surprised he isn't careening off the walls."

"He was doing just that," Enzo said, "for most of the night. He must be exhausted."

"Good time for us to confront him, then," Gunter replied.

"I am not so certain," Enzo said. "Xaviere must be lurking nearby. Unless he has gone on his own hunt and abandoned his pupil."

"Scant chance of that," Jackson said. "He'll be on us the instant we approach Jean-Claude." In fact, he'd come to the realization that was precisely what Legrand had intended.

If he had any sense of self-preservation, Jackson would leave Jean-Claude to his fate and return to the safety of his lair. He didn't want to fight Legrand's second-in-command—the duel would squander the life essence he so desperately needed to fight Legrand himself. When he eventually defeated Europe's master, Jean-Claude would gain his freedom by default.

But what degradations would he be forced to endure in the meantime? It was a dismal reward for Jean-Claude's loyal service to Jackson. Another thought occurred: Dawn was not far off. Legrand may have ordered that Jean-Claude be abandoned to the sun. His agonizing death would serve as warning to any of Legrand's slaves who, like Jackson, dared to escape. Jackson had witnessed many such executions during his own captivity.

No, Jackson couldn't risk leaving Jean-Claude on the streets. Not if he wanted to live with his conscience—and not if he wanted ever again wished to look Solange in the face.

If Jean-Claude was bait...if Xaviere—or Legrand himself—was watching for Jackson's approach, so be it.

"We advance," he said. "Slowly. We can't afford to startle him. The two of you separate and approach him from either end of the alley. I'll descend from here."

His minions accepted his orders without question, fading into the darkness. Jackson crept along the terra cotta roof tiles. He halted at a point directly above Jean-Claude's doorway, at a height of four stories. It was a vantage point that put Jackson's quarry out of view. Crouching, he caught hold of the roof's edge and swung down over the eave, landing on a windowsill on the building's uppermost level.

He'd barely landed when the creak of a door and a cheerful melody of female voices, slightly tipsy, reached his ears. He looked down sharply, to a doorway on the opposite side of the alley, barely a dozen steps from Jean-Claude's hiding place. Three young women had emerged. They paused together on the street, their glossy dark heads nearly touching as they laughed.

Jackson sensed, rather than heard, Jean-Claude stir below him. Enzo appeared at the bend in the alley behind the group of girls, moving as swiftly as he dared. There was no sign of Gunter at the opposite end of the alley, where it gave way to a wider thoroughfare.

Jean-Claude lurched to his feet. Jackson had a clear view of him now. The vampire leaned around the doorframe, his mouth streaked with blood, his clothing soaked in it. He fixed his gaze on the three women.

His eyes began to glow. Jackson swore softly as one woman lifted her head, eyes roaming the alley as if searching for someone who had just called her name.

Jean-Claude's vampire mesmerism, even raw and untutored, was effective. Three pairs of eyes sought and found its source. Jackson sensed Jean-Claude tense, preparing to pounce on the closest woman.

Jackson released his hold on the window's frame. He landed lightly on his feet, little more than an arm's length in front of the women. Arms spread wide, body tensed, he absorbed Jean-Claude's thwarted strike in a brutal blow to his back. The three women remained frozen, mouths open, eyes wide and wild. Jackson growled at the girls. Their only move was to cling more tightly to each other, necks arching to reveal even more of their bare throats. Humans, Jackson thought with some disgust. With such poor instinct for self-preservation, it was a wonder the species survived at all.

Jackson felt Jean-Claude shift. He didn't need to turn to know that the vampire had recovered and was coiling for a second strike.

"Run!" he snarled. "Now!"

The tallest woman recovered first. With a shrill shriek, she turned and scrambled down the alley, dragging her companions behind her. Enzo flattened his body against the wall. The trio stumbled past him and fled.

Jackson twisted as Jean-Claude sprung. The vampire's frenzied blow glanced off Jackson's left shoulder. Enzo sprang to his master's aid. At the same time, two new figures flung themselves into the fray. Gunter, at last.

With Solange.

Jackson let out a foul curse. "I ordered you to stay in the crypt."

Solange spared him the briefest of glances and provided no answer at all. Her husband—streaked with the blood of his human prey—consumed her attention.

"Jean-Claude," she whispered. "Oh, my love, what have they done to you?"

Snarling, he swung about, hands claw-like, fangs bared. Enzo grabbed him by the scruff of the neck as he lunged, squeezing hard as Jean-Claude flailed. Jackson snatched Solange, pinning her to his side with one arm as he fixed her husband with the full force of his mesmeric stare.

Jean-Claude twitched spasmodically; Enzo released his hold, shoving the younger vampire at the wall beside the doorway. Jean-Claude stumbled back, arms spread against the peeling plaster, his eyes trained on Jackson. Solange lifted a hand toward her husband. Though she remained silent, Jackson, with his arm around her, was all too aware of her trembling anguish. He'd hoped to spare her the worst of that emotion.

Again, he had failed.

He urged her to turn her face to his shoulder. She sobbed then, her shoulders shaking as she clung to him. Above him, the night sky was lightening far too quickly for comfort. Dawn was almost here.

"Bring him," he told the others. "Quickly."

"I think not," a quiet voice said.

Jackson spun about, shoving Solange behind him. It was an indictment of his mental state that he hadn't even registered an intruder's approach.

"Xaviere," he said. "Well. I can't say I'm surprised to see you here."

The vampire strolled slowly toward them. Tall and skeletal, thin skin stretched like parchment over his bones, Xaviere had served as Legrand's first deputy for over five hundred years. Jackson was intimately familiar with his twisted mind—Xaviere figured nearly as prominently in Jackson's nightmares as Legrand himself.

Enzo and Gunter shifted slightly, flanking their master. Jackson gestured for his minions to remain still. Legrand's deputy was far more powerful than they. Jackson had no doubt that Xaviere could take both vampires apart without disturbing one dusty hair on his head.

Xaviere halted. "As I am unsurprised to see you, Cabot." His eyes flicked to Jean-Claude. "Such sentiment you hold for creatures barely worth the blood needed feed their worthless bodies. It is positively human of you."

"That is none of your concern."

Jackson was painfully aware of the brightening sky. Jean-Claude was already clutching his eyes, trying to shield them from the dawn. A soft whimper escaped his lips. It took years for a new vampire to build a tolerance to dawn and twilight. Jackson was aware also of Enzo and Gunter's growing agitation. The pair was not nearly as old as Jackson; they would soon need to escape the light.

"You are wrong," Xaviere said, following Jackson's gaze. "This vampire is my personal concern. After all, I made him." He smiled. "He owes me his life."

"He owes you nothing," Jackson stepped closer, drawing Xaviere's gaze as he made a swift gesture behind his back. "But I... Ah, well, that is a different story. I owe you much."

"Yes." Xaviere laughed. The sound was like nails screeching on a blackboard. "How well I remember your days as an infant vampire. You were so pathetically grateful for my tutelage. You followed me on your knees like a dog. You hunted for me, bared your throat to me, drained yourself for me. You even crept into my bed and begged me to—"

Now. Jackson sent the silent command. His steward and minions sprang into action. Enzo heaved Jean-Claude over his shoulder as Solange launched a stream of red deathfire from her fingertips. Gunter shielded her as best he could as the three made their escape.

Jackson landed a blow to the side of Xaviere's head and followed. He had no intention of drawing the older vampire into a duel. Chances were good Jackson would win, but the battle would leave him severely depleted of life essence. As it was, he would need to recover a good deal of strength before he challenged Legrand. If the vampire master didn't find him first.

They surged out of the alley and across the piazza to the building that sheltered an unmapped entrance to Jackson's catacomb lair. The sky was bright enough now to cast the dim shadow of a stone fountain across the cobbles. A distinct glow lit the sky behind the building to the east. Jean-Claude's cheek, turned toward the sun as his head bounced against Enzo's back, blazed a blistering red.

With every second, Jackson expected an assault from behind. It never came. They crossed the piazza without incident, ducking down a basement well choked with trash and through a low doorway. Solange first, then Gunter. Enzo, carrying Jean-Claude, stepped forward.

A dark blur overtook him, bearing the stench of rotted flesh. Enzo let out a cry and clutched at his burden. But Jean-Claude was already gone, snatched by Xaviere.

A ray of sunlight crossed the cobbles; there was no question of Jackson hurtling into the day in pursuit. Sick with remorse, Jackson shoved Enzo through the cellar door and followed. The door clanged shut behind him, closing them all in darkness.

Solange called a ball of red witch light into her trembling hand. Her eyes darted to Enzo, who stood empty-handed, then to Jackson, who could not bring himself to meet her gaze.

"Jean-Claude?" she whispered.

"I am sorry," Jackson said.

Chapter Seven

"I will remain on the surface, monsieur. You must be protected while the sun is high."

Jackson ran a weary hand down his face. Solange stood before him, unnaturally calm, as she always was. Only her red-rimmed eyes betrayed the state of her emotions. Not for the first time, he cursed the dawn.

"I cannot like it," he said at last.

"There is no choice. I must keep watch for Legrand's stewards. There are many powerful sorcerers among them. My wardings will not stand if I am not present to reinforce the spells in the event of a direct attack."

Jackson hesitated. He had already sent Enzo and Gunter to their much-needed rest. He was ready to drop as well—the encounter with Xaviere had taxed his strength more than he liked to admit. He desperately needed the renewal of sleep. But the thought of leaving Solange alone on the surface didn't sit well.

"You will wake me the instant you sense trouble," he said. "Whether it has been five hours, or five minutes."

"Of course."

"Then I will retire."

Solange frowned. "Monsieur...?"

He turned back to her. "Yes?"

"The Sidhe woman, she remains chained to your bed."

"I am well aware." Indeed, he'd thought of little else since his return to the crypt. Leanna, arms bound and spread wide, awaiting his arrival...

"I will sleep elsewhere," he growled.

Solange bowed and disappeared up the crude stairway leading to the surface. He stood motionless for a long moment, staring after her. Then he shook his head slightly, as if to dislodge unwelcome thoughts. Turning, he made his way down the passageway, past humans so long dead their bodies had long ago lost the odor of decay.

Remember, man, that thou art dust...

There were several chambers, cleaned and furnished, which would have been suitable for his rest. He passed each one, not even attempting to fool himself into believing he was headed anywhere but the one place he should avoid. Berating himself as a fool, he traversed the passage leading to his bed and the living woman who lay upon it.

A low moan drifted from beyond the tapestry—a sound of pure misery. Something inside his chest twisted. Grasping the edge of the tapestry, he thrust the heavy brocade aside.

Leanna lay on his bed, arms spread by his chains. She appeared to be asleep. Her eyes were closed, her chest heaving. Her legs were pressed together, drawn up convulsively against her body. Her head tossed from side to side.

"No," she moaned. "No—"

What horror invaded her dreams? With a glance, he noted the brace of candles had burned themselves out. That was little hindrance to his vampiric sight, but to Leanna it would mean total, terrifying darkness. Swiftly, he located the fresh candles Solange kept nearby for her own use. Lighting several, he replaced the exhausted tapers in the stand.

The light dazzled his vision. Crossing swiftly to Leanna's side, he leaned over the bed.

"Leanna," he rasped. "Wake up. Wake up now." Reaching out to her, he cupped one hand on the side of her face. With his thumb, he wiped away her tears.

At his touch, she stilled. She came back to reality slowly, eyes first squeezing tightly, then slowly fluttering open.

"Jackson?"

He sat on the edge of the bed. "I am here."

"I was asleep?"

"Yes."

She searched his gaze, then her lashes swept downward and a shudder ran through her body. "Thank the gods. I...it seemed so real."

"It was only a dream."

"A nightmare. I was...I thought I was back in the death realms."

She bit her lip and fell silent, but he had only to look into her eyes to hear what she would not say.

"I understand," he said quietly. "I understand what it is to be enslaved. I once believed there were atrocities I'd rather die than commit. I was wrong."

"Yes," she whispered. "Yes."

He looked away briefly, while he savored the sensation of her warm skin under his palm. Then he pulled his hand away, and stood.

"Your past is dead," he told her. "Dead and gone." He stood for a moment, looking down at her. Then he sighed and turned away. "Return to your rest. I will light more candles and leave them burning. They will last until I return at dusk."

"No!" The raw panic in her voice had him turning back to her, though he knew it was the last thing he should do.

"You can't mean to leave me again," she pleaded. "Not like this. Unchain me, at least."

"Only to have you escape while I sleep?"

"No, I promise I won't. I'll stay right here until you return."

He smiled grimly. "Much as I'd like to, Leanna, I'm afraid I can't trust you. Too much is at stake. Now more than ever, since..." He fell silent.

"Since what?"

"Nothing."

"It's not nothing. You look horrible—and exhausted. What happened on the surface? Did you find Jean-Claude?"

"Yes, we found him."

"And—?"

"There was...a spot of trouble."

"Legrand?"

"No. Legrand's deputy, Xaviere. He set Jean-Claude on his blood rampage." He paused. "Which was every bit as bad as I feared."

"Well. At least now you know your friend isn't dead."

"Not dead?" Jackson laughed. "Oh, make no mistake, Leanna. Jean-Claude is most certainly dead. Worse than dead, in fact." He clenched his fist. "He is a monster. He ripped out the throats of at least six humans. Most likely more."

She bit her lip. "Were you able to bring him back with you?"

Jackson looked away. He spread his fingers only to immediately form them into a fist again. "No. I failed in his rescue."

"Oh, Jackson! I'm so sorry."

"No more so than I. So you see, Leanna, you've become even more precious to me. I must defeat Legrand very soon, if I'm to have any hope of rescuing Jean-Claude before his mind cracks under the horror of what he's become. Your magic is the best chance I have."

She shuddered. "I was a death magic addict, Jackson. The thought of having sex with Legrand sickens me. But even so, I'm afraid once I get a taste of his vampire magic, I'll beg him for it. I'm afraid that once he touches me, he'll make me want to have sex with him. I may even enjoy it."

The expression in her eyes was unutterably bleak. "Please, Jackson," she whispered. "Don't make me do it. There has to be another way. Let me call Mac. I can convince him to help you—I know I can."

Jackson only wished he had Leanna's unwavering faith in her brother. Unfortunately, he was not so sanguine. Death magic wasn't synonymous with evil, any more than light magic was synonymous with good. An equal measure of each type of magic made life on Earth possible. Many death magic creatures acted honorably and many life magic creatures did not. However, the past century had taught Jackson that life magic creatures were prone to bigotry. They believed themselves better than their death magic counterparts, whom they held in contempt. The situation hadn't been aided by the fact that a depraved demon had recently nearly succeeded in his plan to permanently upset the balance of magic and obliterate all life on Earth.

There would be no help from Leanna's demigod brother. Oh, Jackson didn't doubt Mac would come for his sister in an instant. But he wouldn't stick around long enough to even hear about Jackson's dilemma, much less offer aid. No matter how eloquently Leanna pleaded, the great Manannán mac Lir would not lift a finger to aid any vampire, let alone one who had kidnapped his sister out of her bed.

No, Jackson knew there was only one way forward if he were to destroy Legrand and rescue Jean-Claude, and that chance hinged on his delivering Leanna into

Legrand's clutches. Unfortunately, staring down into her wide, tear-wet eyes, another unwelcome certainty struck him.

He could not do it.

Leanna was a creature of light. A woman who, after having lost her way in darkness and evil for so many years, had finally found the path to happiness and goodness. Who was he to kill all her living hope, to smother all her love and warmth with the hatred of his cold, dead heart?

No, he could not do it. He *would* not. And because Jackson had suddenly turned up weak, Jean-Claude would exist in terror and degradation for years, perhaps decades. Solange's grief would remain raw and Jackson would know her sorrow was his fault.

The weight of his failure threatened to crush him. His knees begin to buckle. He was tired, so tired. His disordered thoughts spun as he sat down heavily on the edge of his bed. He was only dimly aware that the misery on Leanna's face had been replaced by an expression of deep concern.

"Jackson? What is it? Are you unwell?"

Half-turning, he gazed at her. He should release her now, urge her to leave him, but he couldn't bear the thought of falling into the sleep he so desperately needed, only to wake alone.

"I need rest," he told her. "That's all."

Avoiding her eyes, he released the leather cuff from her right wrist and unlocked both chains from the bedpost. Weighing the chain that still bound her left arm, he snapped the metal handcuff on its other end around his own right wrist.

Leanna's brow furrowed. "Jackson?"

He lay down and reached for her. His eyes closed; he felt oblivion tugging him toward darkness. But it wasn't the cold, dead darkness he was accustomed to. It was warm and—despite his utter lack of faith in his future—hopeful.

"Jackson?" Leanna's breath brushed his ear. "What are you doing?"

"Sleeping with you," he murmured.

Chapter Eight

A short time later, Leanna lay awake. Jackson still slept, his arm a pleasant weight encircling her torso. The hard length of his body, slightly cool, pressed against her back. The chain that had tethered her to his bed now tethered him to her. She suspected that even if it were unlocked and discarded, they would both still feel its presence.

She released tentative tendrils of life magic in his direction. He stirred, moving closer, like a flower turning with the sun. Slowly, she rolled until she lay facing him, the chain coiled between them. She slipped her arms around his neck and kissed him.

His breathing did not change but his eyes opened. He lay silent for a moment, not reacting. She leaned close and kissed him again.

"You smell like sunshine," he said. "Like green grass in the sun, or a clear stream with diamond lights reflecting on its surface. Like white clouds, floating on a blue sky."

"Oh, Jackson."

"All the things I'll never see again." He drew back. "You need to leave me, Leanna, before I do you irreparable damage."

"You would never hurt me."

He laughed, harshly. "You think not? You're a fool. I can hurt you all too easily. I can be nothing but death to you."

"I don't believe that. I won't believe it."

"You know, I can hear your heart beating quite clearly. The life blood pumping through your veins arouses me. I want to taste it, drink deeply, take it for myself."

Leanna sat up, and regarded him steadily, uncertain of Jackson's new, strangely poignant mood. "I want to give it to you." *Because I love you.* But she didn't say the words.

She laid a hand on his arm. "Make love with me, Jackson."

"No," he said swiftly. "Absolutely not." But he didn't pull back.

"Don't you trust me? Do you think I'd use my muse magic against you?"

"That's not it." He shoved himself off the bed. He fumbled with the cuff on his wrist until, finally, with a faint click, the lock opened. Bending forward, he grabbed her wrist and freed it as well. The chain dropped to the ground as he took a step back and shoved both hands in his pockets. "We cannot have sex, Leanna."

Her gaze dropped to where the fabric of his trousers strained over his erection.

"I think we can," she said softly.

His lips drew back, revealing fully extended incisors. His eyes bled midnight. "Be careful what you ask for, my dear. Sex with a vampire invariably ends in blood."

"I want that, too." Gods help her, it was true. She craved his bite. She wanted to belong to him in every way possible.

"You don't know what you're saying. I'm a monster."

"You're not. You're an honorable man."

"Like hell." He yanked his hands from his pockets and advanced on her so quickly she had no chance at all to react. Gripping her shoulders, he dragged her body against his.

She went very still as he lowered his head. His lips grazed her neck. He nipped at her. His fangs scraped, but not deeply enough to break her skin. Not yet.

His mouth was hot on her neck, his breathing labored. "You are a fool to want me, Leanna. You think you know what I've become, what I'm capable of. You don't. You have no idea."

"Show me. I'll decide for myself."

He hesitated. Then, with a low growl, he gathered her dress in his hands and yanked the fabric to her waist. Cold hands roamed her heated skin. When he explored between her thighs, she moaned at the contact. She was slick, so ready for him. He grunted, a low, guttural sound, barely human. For the first time, waves of trepidation overtook Leanna. She swiftly banished her doubts. This was Jackson. She had to believe he wouldn't hurt her. When his hand moved again, she parted her legs.

Moving. Turning. Falling. Somehow she ended up with her spine pressed to the bed. Jackson stood over her, his handsome face shadowed—strained—filling her vision. She lifted her arms to him. He didn't move. He held himself rigid at the foot of the bed, holding himself apart from her. His breathing was ragged. His hands were fisted, his knuckles white.

She stared up at him, panting, needing, wanting him so badly. She was ready to do anything for him, even damn her own soul. He stood over her, motionless, his gaze so hot and desperate it seared her skin.

His body trembled. He wanted her, she knew, though perhaps he didn't want to need her. *I love you*, she longed to say. *I've always loved you*. But she doubted he would believe her. And so she lay still and silent as he held himself apart and devoured her with his eyes.

His gaze lit a trail of fire down her body, pausing at her most sensitive spots. Every pulse point became a throbbing center of pleasure. Her neck, her wrists, the inside of her elbows. The back of her knees. The crease at the top of her thighs, the dark place between her legs.

The aching sensations pulsed together, lifting her, opening her. It took a moment for her to realize that as much as she wanted him, this blissful torment wasn't entirely natural. It was magic. Dark magic. Jackson was creating this dark need, this overwhelming want, this craving for her own surrender. That was, after all, what vampires did.

Her gaze jerked to his. The vulnerability she'd thought she'd glimpsed there had vanished. A chill cascaded down her spine.

He smiled grimly. "If I can't change your mind with words, then, as you've asked, I'll show you. This is what I am, Leanna. A vampire. Unliving, unfeeling. I take what I want. I give death in return."

A terrifying wave of longing swept over her. How she craved his death magic! Quickly in the wake of her desire, trepidation ensued. Was this all just Jackson's revenge? Did he tempt her deliberately with death magic, as she'd so often tempted her lovers with her muse magic? Were the exquisite feelings coursing through her body nothing but a revival of her past obsession with death? Was she any different from any vampire addict, in any seedy back room of any vampire club, in any city in the world?

She longed to believe that her feelings for Jackson were not the product of addiction. That they were pure, good, and beautiful. Once, they'd shared a great love. But that was in the past. The man she'd once loved was gone. Jackson's eyes were blank and bitter. His were not the eyes of a lover, but those of a predator.

Leanna felt ill. She tried to close her legs. He wouldn't allow it. Her hips, riding on the wave of his death magic, lifted toward him. Her body was weeping for him, wanting him inside. Craving death. Craving *him*. Craving the man he'd once been; the man she'd loved.

The man she had killed.

The wet silk of her thong felt raw against the dark, building pleasure. Grim satisfaction shone in Jackson's eyes. "Do you see now, Leanna? This is what I am. How does it feel, to surrender control of your body, your mind, your very soul, to a vampire?"

"Like Heaven," she whispered. "Like Heaven and Hell, together."

"Damn you..."

Pleasure fell on her body like a jailer's whip. Jackson flogged her with bliss, over and over. There was nothing but shame in this kind of punishment, but the deeper Leanna fell, the less she cared. Wicked yearning pounded her, drenched her, pulled her apart. She was the shore to Jackson's angry ocean. She did not try to resist. The shore did not run from the sea.

The tide of sensation lifted her, tossed her, used her. She writhed, her palms flat on the mattress near her hips, as if someone held them pinned. All the time she kept her eyes open, staring up at Jackson.

He still hadn't so much as laid a finger on her.

His breathing was harsh. Beads of sweat formed on his forehead, ran down his face. His fangs shone in the faint light. She had never seen anything so beautiful.

She was close to climax, so close, but the peak eluded her.

"Jackson. Please. Touch me. Come inside me."

His jaw clenched so tightly she thought it would snap. A vein pulsed in his temple. Yearning—deep, elemental longing—flashed in his eyes. He tore open his trousers.

His cock sprang, pale and huge, into his hand. He gripped it so hard Leanna was sure he'd caused himself pain. But the harsh moan that tore from his throat told of a different kind of agony.

She watched him stroke himself. For her. The thought ratcheted up her own arousal. Her hips canted forward. Her gasps mingled with his ragged breath. The sight of his self-pleasure, the hard planes of his body, the taut lines of his face as he milked his shaft, was so beautiful, beyond erotic. But gods, how she wanted him closer.

And then he was kneeling over her, on the bed. So close.

Bliss.

He stroked himself with one hand, touched her with the other. He explored her body almost angrily, igniting fire on her skin. She tried to reach for him. He held himself back; her fingers clutched air. She arched her spine, offering her body. He kneaded her breasts, clawed past her belly, ground the heel of his hand into her mound. He snapped the elastic of her thong and threw the scrap of silk aside. Cool fingers slipped inside her, then withdrew, leaving her shifting and panting with want.

The blunt tip of his erection nudged the entrance to her body. Her eyes clashed with his.

"Come inside," she whimpered. "Please. I need you."

"Damn you," he said. "Damn you to Hell."

His thrust was sure and deep, lifting her half off the bed. His invasion was wonderful beyond bearing. Stars burst behind Leanna's eyes. She clutched at the covers and held on as his hips enacted a hard, almost savage rhythm.

It was too much. He was inside her, around her, too close to all the feelings she'd repressed for decades. The vulnerability attacked her control over her powers. She tried to keep tight rein on her muse magic, but somehow, despite her intentions, it had escaped, and Jackson had become entangled by it. Her power flowed to him as her orgasm shattered.

Another vow broken. It should have felt wrong, but it did not. It felt right, like coming home after a long, lonely journey.

Jackson's body went tense. With a shout, he emptied himself inside her. His was dead seed, she knew. Seed that would never grow.

But somehow, the wet heat of it felt like new life.

Chapter Nine

The shout that erupted from Jackson's lips at the instant of his release was equal parts bliss and rage. The orgasm—his first in nearly three-quarters of a century—ripped through his brain with the vicious strength of a ravening beast. Seven decades of ruthless self-control, obliterated in one long groan of ecstasy.

How could he be this close to Leanna's muse magic and not touch it? True to her word, she held her power tightly in check, making no demands on his life essence. Unfortunately, was all too aware of the utter bliss that awaited him should he possess it.

He remembered only too well the first time he'd tasted her magic in Paris. Every time before, when they'd made love, she had kept the heart of her magic apart from him. But that glorious morning, for the first time, she'd allowed him the privilege of touching it. For several beautiful, spinning hours, his spirit had soared on the wings of her creative inspiration. He'd seen so clearly the perfect colors and textures of the masterpiece. He'd seen—*known*—how simple it would be to transform paint and canvas into genius.

His fingers closed convulsively on an invisible paintbrush. How easy it had been, that first time, to succumb to the temptation she'd extended. How foolish he'd been to accept a viper's gift. His trusting heart had led him down a twisted path to death and enslavement.

He was not that innocent youth. He was an undead monster. He was no longer fooled by Leanna's magic. He knew it as the trap that it was.

He knew it, and yet, he'd ignored his hard-won knowledge. Again, he'd reached for her magic. This time, she held it apart from him, but it hardly mattered. He was strong enough now to take what he wanted. This time, he told himself, her power couldn't kill him—he was already vampire, already dead.

He looked down at her. He was still buried inside her, and her face bore the wonder of their joining. His dead heart clenched, painfully. Life, love, art, purpose. He thought a century of death had erased the memory of these virtues, but now, against all odds, he felt them once again. Had he imagined time could obliterate his love for this woman? It had not. He'd loved her once. And—God help him—he loved her still. And for the sake of that emotion he'd been willing to worship at the altar of her magic.

Enthralled as he was in this perfect moment of blissful purpose, he wasn't immediately aware that his hoarded life essence was seeping from his bones and sinews like water from a sieve. His awareness built slowly, along with a rising, sickening horror as his power slid away through the bliss. His loss accelerated dangerously, coming perilously close to hemorrhage before he managed to completely wrench his mind from Leanna's muse magic.

Once his mind was again his own, the flow of his life essence slowed to a trickle, then halted entirely. Appalled and still dazed, sick at heart, Jackson struggled to assess how much life potency he'd squandered. A year's worth? Ten years? More? Had he, in a fit of weak sentimentality, doomed himself to another fifty years of playing cat and mouse with Legrand?

Caught as he was between a fading edge of pleasure and the sickening knowledge of what he'd lost, Jackson didn't notice the trembling of the cavern walls until Leanna's startled cry jerked his attention back to his surroundings. A loud crack split the air. A chunk of rock, then a shower of pebbles and grit, rained down all around.

Leanna coughed, scrambling upright and shoving down her dress. "Gods, Jackson! The roof—"

He looked up and saw several jagged cracks in the rock, lengthening and widening before his eyes. "Son of a—"

He grabbed Leanna's arm and yanked her off the bed. An instant later, a section of the catacomb ceiling crashed onto the mattress where they'd lain just seconds before. He lost control of their backward momentum; they landed together on the carpet in a tangle of limbs. Instinctively, he rolled, sheltering Leanna with his body as more debris cascaded from the shattered ceiling.

Something struck his arm, clung, and burned. Biting back a curse, his eyes shot toward the pain. He expected to see flames, but his arm wasn't on fire at all. It was bathed in sunlight.

His gaze jerked upward. Blue sky gaped through a yawning hole in the catacomb ceiling. The edges of the gap were still crumbling, admitting even more destructive light. Jackson lay at the edge of a brilliant pool of daylight.

"Damnation." He scrambled out of the sun's path, dragging a senseless Leanna with him. Her eyes were closed. Blood trickled from a gash on her forehead. He froze for an instant, staring at the jagged crimson line. He wanted, more than anything, to drag his tongue through that wet stream of life.

Instead he forced himself to crawl to darkness. Once clear of the sun, Jackson sat for a moment, cradling Leanna in his lap, breathing through the pain of his burned arm. His eyes were drawn backward, toward the glorious shaft of light he'd fled. It pierced the gloom of the catacomb like an avenging angel's sword. Swirls of white dust danced on the blade.

Apprehension bled into his gut. Where was Solange? If the cave-in had been natural, she would have already appeared in the light, looking for him. That she had not was a very bad sign.

He would give much to be able to leap into the sun and call to her. But that was impossible. He cursed his impotence. He could feel his face reddening, just from the ambient light. His wounded arm burned. His eyes stung.

Even worse was how the sun had churned his emotions. The kiss of sunlight had stripped his soul bare. He felt as weak and naked as a newly made vampire, cowering in agony before a single slender candle.

The memory of Legrand's laughter echoed in his skull. Legrand took particular delight in a new slave's agony.

Don't think of the past. Think of here and now.

His arms tightened on the woman in his arms.

"Leanna?"

No answer; she was still unconscious. He half-carried, half-dragged her farther from the light. The movement woke her. Thank the gods. Her eyelids fluttered open.

She focused on his face with dazed eyes. "What...happened?"

"The catacomb ceiling caved in. A chunk of it hit you on the head."

"I feel...dizzy."

"Don't worry. I'll take care of you." Jackson's knees shook as he rose; he was grateful his legs didn't buckle entirely. Slogging through rubble, he made his way toward the tapestry that formed the far wall of his ruined sanctuary. If he could just get to the other side, where the sun couldn't follow, he might be able to quell his rising panic long enough to consider his next move.

He feared Legrand's human minions had engineered the cave's collapse. Had the bastards harmed Solange? Had they taken her? He couldn't bear the thought. And what of Enzo and Gunter? Jackson's vampires were stationed nearer to the catacomb's entrance. They should have been at his side by now, unless they'd also met with an attack.

He shoved the tapestry aside with one shoulder and ducked behind it. His blood froze at the sound of a harsh Gallic voice. Jackson went rigid, his eyes fixed on the figure stepping from the shadows.

"*Bonjour,* Monsieur Cabot." A glint of white teeth accompanied a rasping voice. "At last, I have cornered the rabbit in his lair. He now faces the sharp jaws of the fox. The master will be most pleased."

Jackson's jaw clenched. "Go to the devil, Xaviere."

Leanna twisted in his arms, eyes widening as they took in the intruder. Jackson lowered her body to the ground, setting her on her feet.

"Go," he whispered urgently. "Escape. He cannot follow you into the light."

Her grip on his upper arms tightened.

Xaviere's small eyes flicked over Leanna, then returned to Jackson. The vampire smiled thinly.

"You are surprised, *mon ami*, that I would hunt you while the sun shines? Ah, but you should not be. Night has not provided good hunting where you are concerned. You are far too clever for your tender years. But your minions...the two in the tunnels? They are young and foolish. And now they are...gone."

"You lie."

"Do I?" Xaviere opened his fist. A slow stream of ash poured through his fingers.

Jackson caught a fleeting whiff of Gunter's scent, then Enzo's. He closed his eyes briefly on a surge of grief.

"Your young steward on the surface is very clever. But not, alas, clever enough. She gave her best, but..." His shoulders lifted and fell. "*C'est la vie*, no? Or perhaps, more accurately...*c'est la mort*? For she will be dead soon enough."

Jackson felt ill. Shame and grief struck like a physical blow. "You and Legrand will pay for what you've done if it's the last action I take in this world."

Xaviere's fangs flashed. "I think not, *mon jeune ami*. But I tell you this: your witch fought bravely. I am sure the master will enjoy reuniting her with her unfortunate husband."

"I will take them back," Jackson hissed.

"Come now, Cabot. Do you not weary of this game? You cannot win. You cannot hide from your master forever. Sooner or later, Legrand will drive you to your knees." The vampire laughed. "You have been there before. If you beg sweetly and perform well, he may be moved to tolerate your continued existence."

Jackson barely heard the taunts. His mind burned with the image of Solange in Legrand's hands, delivered there through her loyalty to Jackson. Why had he allowed her to serve him? He should have sent her away when her grandfather died.

Leanna touched his arm. He felt her surge of empathy. He didn't want to turn, didn't want to look at her. Would his pride, his pitiful craving for human contact, destroy her as well? Damn it, why wouldn't she run? He angled his body, shielding her from Xaviere's view.

The vampire's amused gaze slipped to a spot below Jackson's waist. Belatedly, Jackson realized his trousers were still undone from his encounter with Leanna. With a muttered curse, he jerked up the zipper.

Xaviere's teeth glinted. "Ah," he said now. "I understand the cause of your inattention. I admit, I did not expect you to be...entertaining...when I came for you. Did you imagine your sanctuary to be inviolate? Your power may be far beyond what a vampire of your years should wield, Cabot, but soon you will know your rightful place. Legrand will render you weak as a cub."

"Legrand can go to Hell."

"Undoubtedly, he will. Eventually. But not, I think, today. Today belongs to you." Xaviere paced a step closer. "You may believe yourself to be a match for me, but I am far older, far stronger. Your game is up, Cabot. I am here to crush you."

He might very well succeed. Jackson struggled to mask the deadening fatigue dragging at his limbs. His knees were trembling. He wasn't precisely sure how much magic he could currently bring to bear in a fight, but one thing was certain. Xaviere was aware of Jackson's weakness. A small smile played on the vampire's lips.

Jackson contemplated his chances of surviving a duel. Xaviere was not as powerful as Legrand. Even an hour before, Jackson was sure he would have defeated the deputy with little trouble. Now he couldn't even count on holding his own.

As if sensing the direction of his thoughts, Leanna stepped from behind him to stand at his side. Xaviere's cool gaze slid over her.

"A Sidhe," he said. "How very interesting. The master will enjoy her."

The taunt snapped Jackson's control. The thought of Legrand's hands on Leanna... He lunged at his enemy's sneering face. The sudden attack caught Xaviere by surprise. Jackson slammed the vampire's skull into the wall behind him. His fingers found Xaviere's throat and squeezed.

But the precious seconds of advantage didn't last. Cursing, Xaviere threw Jackson back. Jackson kept his grip on the vampire's throat, dragging Xaviere with him. The pair staggered in a grotesque dance, spinning then lurching heavily against the free-hanging tapestry. The billowing carpet broke their fall.

Jackson grabbed one edge of the weighty fabric as he fell. The tapestry tore from its ceiling hooks, falling amid a shower of dusty grit. Jackson went down. Xaviere fell atop him. The vampire's knee cracked against Jackson's sternum, driving the air from his lungs.

He choked as his foe sprang to his feet. Xaviere grabbed the front of Jackson's shirt, lifting him, one handed, into the air. With a brutal heave, he flung Jackson in the direction of the sunlight.

Jackson grabbed the edge of the table just in time to halt his deadly forward momentum. The heavy furniture toppled; Jackson ducked behind it. As he dropped to his knees, he caught a glimpse of Leanna, scrambling over the debris piled atop his shattered bed. She entered the light. Her pale dress shone like an angel's robe.

Go, he urged silently. *Escape.*

She paused near the gap in the cavern roof. She was a short jump to freedom—why was she stopping?

An instant later, Jackson understood. Two hulking figures were climbing through the opening, framed by daylight. Legrand's human minions. Leanna hadn't been bent on escape. God in Heaven! She meant to defend him.

She uttered a stream of words in a strange language. It sounded like a battle cry. Her fingers traced a pattern in the air. Elfshot exploded. A man's howling cry told Jackson she'd hit her mark. His large body fell, impacting the cavern floor with a resounding thud.

Then Xaviere loomed large, blocking Jackson's view of Leanna's battle. The vampire slashed; his claws whistled. Jackson defensive move didn't come quickly enough. Sharp nails opened a gash on his throat.

Blood spurted; life energy hemorrhaged. Crimson puddled on the cavern floor.

Laughing, Xaviere closed his fingers around Jackson's neck. More blood splashed. Xaviere's claws twisted, and Jackson gagged. Vertebrae in his neck popped.

He pulled desperately at Xaviere's hands. When the iron claws wouldn't bend, he tried to get his own fingers around the vampire's neck. But Xaviere was taller, his arms longer. Jackson couldn't get enough leverage.

Xaviere's eyes flashed dark with satisfaction. *"C'est fini,* Cabot. The end. My only regret is that the master is not here to witness your destruction."

"I'm sure you will console him," Jackson choked out. "I'm sure you will bend over and offer Legrand your—"

He gagged as Xaviere's fist crushed his windpipe. Oxygen ceased to flow into Jackson's lungs. It was an odd sensation, not breathing. But hardly fatal. A vampire did not need to breathe.

But a vampire did need blood, and Jackson's body was leaking copious amounts of that precious commodity. The edge of his vision went fuzzy. Raw survival instinct kicked in; he lashed out with all his strength. But all his strength wasn't good enough.

Xaviere was stronger. And for that, Jackson had only himself to blame.

He could no longer see Leanna—had she defeated the other human minions and fled to safety? He fervently hoped so. If she was safe, he could die with a measure of peace.

Peace. At last.

He closed his eyes and offered a prayer for his damned soul. He did not think God would hear him, much less answer, but the habits of childhood died hard.

Xaviere's laugh echoed. His grip on Jackson's neck tightened, Jackson's stolen blood pumped into the dirt. There was an odd sound, a ringing in his ears, a strange melody he'd never before heard. Light flashed into his vision.

The end had come. He only hoped it would be swift.

Chapter Ten

Leanna's spell slammed Xaviere right between the shoulder blades.

It was perhaps the most powerful binding charm she'd ever crafted. The result was swift and supremely satisfying. The vampire's body went rigid. His legs stiffened; his knees locked. His fingers snapped open and his arms flung wide. He teetered for one long second before toppling, face first, onto the ground.

The bind was a life-magic spell, unable to kill. But with sunlight streaming through the shattered catacomb ceiling and Xaviere unable to move, it would be easy enough to drag him into the light and finish him off. So much for the vows she'd made in Annwyn. All her promises, all her good intentions, had gone up in flames. Three of Legrand's human stewards already lay dead. Leanna shoved her guilt to the back of her mind. She'd examine her crimes later.

After she finished committing them.

She scrambled down the pile of rocks on the bed, half sliding, half falling, scraping her shin in her haste to reach Jackson's side. He lay in a puddle of blood, his neck bearing a cruel slash and the deep imprint of Xaviere's fingers. He wasn't breathing, and she couldn't find a pulse. If he were mortal, he'd be dead. But Jackson was vampire. The normal rules didn't apply.

Dirt trickled onto her head. Startled, she looked up. A clump of grass—and a dead man's limp arm—hung over the edge of the hole, framed by a patch of blue sky. She held her breath, but there was no shout, no sound other than the distant hum of traffic. But surely there were more of Legrand's minions about.

If she was going to escape, now was the time.

She rejected the thought even as it formed. Jackson had urged her to run, but she had no intention of leaving him. She eyed Xaviere's motionless form. First things first.

Grabbing the vampire's ankles, she tugged his body toward the light. He was heavy; she conjured a spell to assist. Even so, she grunted as she heaved the undead corpse onto the pool of daylight on Jackson's carpet.

Bright sun bathed Xaviere's face. In an instant, his skin reddened to lobster hue, then darkened to the color of old blood. Leanna watched in horror as the blistered skin turned black, curled away from the white skull beneath, and crumbled like ash. Muscles and bones deteriorated next, causing shirt and trousers to deflate like a leaking balloon. In the end, all that was left of Xaviere was dust, a puff of smoke, and a sound like a human sigh.

At last, Leanna averted her eyes. She tried to draw air into her lungs; the breath was painful. She didn't regret what she'd done. It was all too easy to imagine Jackson's beautiful body meeting the same horrible end. Turning her back on the sight, she made her way to Jackson's side.

He lay just beyond the farthest reaches of the sun. His normally pale skin was red and blistered. Gods, the sun. The angle of the beam had changed, moving the shaft of light across the floor in Jackson's direction. Hooking her hands under his armpits, she dragged him into a narrow side passage of the catacomb, scattering debris as she went. Navigating a dim corridor flanked by ancient tombs and moldy corpses, she didn't stop until she'd turned a sharp corner and the sun was no longer visible.

She illuminated the space with a ball of elflight. Immediately, she wished she hadn't. She'd dragged Jackson through piles of broken bones, many marked by rodent teeth. The trail was slick with his blood. A sheen of white dust coated his clothes and face.

He lay as motionless as a corpse. Panic battered Leanna's ribs; she swallowed it back. Jackson wasn't dead. Or rather, he was dead, but he hadn't left her. A vampire had phenomenal powers of healing, as long as his undead heart remained beating. Jackson would awaken. But when? She sent nervous glances up and down the corridor. More of Legrand's lackeys could attack at any moment. Living stewards could invade from the surface. Vampires could erupt from the depths of the catacombs.

"Jackson."

She laid a hand on the side of his face. His skin was cold. The burn caused by the sun was already fading. She told herself his pallor was a good sign.

"Jackson, can you hear me? Wake up. Please."

No answer, but she thought his chest might have moved. She laid her palm on it and held her breath.

His ribs expanded. Contracted. Ever so slightly. His next inhale was deeper. The next exhale longer. She felt a weak thump against her palm. His heart, still pumping. She watched, stunned, as the raw edges of his neck wound drew together, until the slash was little more than a thin red line. His store of life essence must be vast. Thank the gods for that.

Leanna released the air from her lungs in a long, heartfelt sigh.

Seconds passed. Jackson's eyelids fluttered open. His eyes were glassy, his gaze uncomprehending. Lines creased his forehead.

"Leanna." He licked his lips. "You're...still here." He paused. Swallowed thickly. "Why?"

"Because this is where I want to be. With you."

"Xaviere?"

Leanna drew a sharp breath. "He...the sun hit him. He's...gone."

"The sun...you should have left me. You should have escaped."

She blinked back tears. "I will never escape you, Jackson. Never."

He tried to lift his head, winced, and laid it back down again, stirring a puff of dust.

"Legrand's stewards? Did they return to the surface?"

"No. I...killed them."

Some of the tension seeped from Jackson's body. "Good."

"More will come."

"Yes, certainly."

"We have to get out of here. Can you stand, do you think?"

"I can try." Jackson levered himself onto one elbow. His arm shook. "God."

With effort, he shoved himself into a sitting position. Once upright, he put his head between his knees and groaned.

Leanna watched him closely. "Are you all right?"

"Yes. Comparatively speaking. But I'm weak." He looked up at her, his expression pained. "It's been a long time since I felt so drained. Not since the last time we—" He averted his gaze. "It will take some time for me to regain my strength."

"I'll stay with you."

"No, you—" He cut off abruptly. His next words were spoken so quietly she almost missed them. "How many lovers have you had since our time in Paris, Leanna?"

The non-sequitur took Leanna aback. Heat rushed to her cheeks. "I...I don't know."

He closed his eyes. "Too many to count, I imagine."

It was an accurate assessment. Leanna had had many, many men in the last century. Quite a few had been artists. She'd provided them with magical inspiration; they'd given up their lives for it. But their offerings hadn't made her feel alive. Only Jackson had done that.

"What about you, Jackson? Vampires are hardly famous for their sexual restraint. You must have had hundreds of women in the past century."

"There were many in my early years as a vampire. Men, too. Legrand chose each victim and I could not refuse to perform. I used them. Often, I killed them afterward." His voice sounded infinitely weary. "There is so much blood on my hands, Leanna. A new vampire's craving...you cannot imagine how it twists the mind. I would have done anything for blood in those years. Anything. The crimes I committed will land me in Hell for all eternity."

"You had no choice."

"Not at first, no. But then...my vampire power started to grow. More and more, I was able to assert my own will. Choose the time, the place, the victim. My crimes became my own. For years, I did not let myself feel the full horror of what I had become. But then, one night, I did feel it. And it nearly destroyed me."

"Oh, Jackson."

"Twenty-five years after my turning, I was no better than any of Legrand's worst minions. And then...I found the courage to forge my own path."

"How?"

His eyes fixed on a point beyond her right shoulder. "It was May. I remember that most clearly. Springtime in Paris, like the one you and I had shared, with lilacs blooming everywhere. I could see them only at night, of course, when the light was gone and colors muted, but the scent...it haunted me. My grandmother had grown lilacs in her garden. That spring, under the lilacs, I discovered she had died."

His lips twisted. "I'd hired an investigator to bring me news of my family. They believed me dead. As indeed I was. I was my grandmother's favorite. She never fully recovered from my loss. The day after I learned of her death, as I slept in Legrand's cellar, I dreamed of her. The image was so vivid. So real. So...alive. When I woke, I felt almost human. That night, the time came to roam, to kill. Yes, I took blood. I can't reject the bloodthirst entirely without destroying myself. But I drank only a little from each woman, took only as much as I needed. Afterward, I made sure my victim forgot what had happened. But as for my carnal needs—I did not fulfill them. I returned to my coffin at dawn, still wanting."

His laugh was weak. "The next evening I woke much stronger than the evening before. After a month of abstinence, I became a thousand times more powerful. I realized then that sexual energy was a form of life essence—life essence a vampire typically wastes in degenerate sex. I wondered if, in repressing my craving for orgasm, I could horde that energy and use it to strengthen my power. All around me, other vampires squandered their sexual essence. Legrand most of all. His vast sexual appetite keeps his power from growing, but he does not notice, or perhaps he does not care. Legrand is the oldest in Europe—his power is vast. It's been decades since he faced a serious challenger. Even so, that night I vowed I would destroy him."

"How long ago was that?"

"Seventy-three years."

"And in all that time—?" Leanna's whispered question hung between them.

"I haven't had a woman. Even without a partner, I haven't experienced an orgasm. Until today, with you."

A horrifying thought struck. "And during our...encounter, I felt you entangled in my magic. Did I imagine that? Or was it real?"

"It was real."

"Oh, gods. Did I drain your life essence?"

"Not you. It was my fault entirely. I took what you had not offered." He grimaced. "And all the blood I lost in battle hasn't helped matters." His gaze traveled the crimson path on the cavern floor. "I don't think I can even stand, much less walk. It will take some time for me to gather enough energy to leave this place."

"You would strengthen faster if you drank blood."

He did not meet her gaze. "Yes."

Yes.

How, Leanna wondered, could one spoken word convey such depths of bitterness. Of self-loathing? Of pure self-disgust?

Her heart nearly broke. With that single syllable, Jackson had revealed more of himself and his undead existence than she suspected he'd meant to. He hated what he was. Utterly. And yet there was no escape.

"You have nothing to be ashamed of, Jackson."

"You think not? I beg to differ. Leave me, Leanna. Leave now."

"I'll do no such—" She broke off as a tendril of death magic snaked through the air, lodging in her chest as an uncomfortable pressure. Someone—something—was approaching. She cocked her head, listening. Feeling with her magic. Ominous vibrations traveled from the ground into her body.

Jackson's breath was harsh, his tone urgent. He'd felt the subtle signs of an intruder, too. "Vampires. Legrand's minions. They'll be on us soon, Leanna. Turn and run. There's still time for you to escape."

"What about you?"

"I can hold them off until you reach daylight."

"Forget it." Leanna was already on her feet. "When Sidhe don't want to be seen, they're not. I can hide us. They'll never know we're here."

Deftly, she wove the strands of a glamour spell, and cast it around Jackson and herself. Sinking to her knees by his side, she commanded the elflight around them to fade into darkness.

"Don't move," she cautioned. "Don't speak."

She felt Jackson's pride prickle. He didn't want to hide from his enemies; despite his weakened state, he wanted to fight them. She wrapped the magical protection tighter and pressed her body against his. He was so cold. So very cold. Her own heart froze with dread.

Three dark shapes appeared at the end of the passage. Eyes glowing with dark light, they muttered among themselves in French as they made their way toward Jackson and Leanna's hiding place.

"The bastard's got to be here. We've blocked all the exits. Xaviere staked Cabot's two pathetic minions—"

Jackson tensed. Leanna tightened her arms around him.

"There's nowhere for him to hide," a second voice muttered. "We've searched every passage. This one is a dead end."

"And yet...he's eluded us. And Xaviere has disappeared as well."

"Perhaps he's captured Cabot."

"And taken him where? Into the light?"

The trio passed within inches of Leanna's right foot, still muttering. They paused at the turn in the passageway, peering toward the sun. Then the lead vampire jumped back, as if stung.

"Dust," he said. "Ash."

"Cabot?" his companions rasped.

The leader advanced a few cautious steps, sniffing the air. A low growl emerged from his throat. "*Merde!* No, not Cabot. Xaviere."

More curses pierced the gloom.

"The master will hold us responsible." Fear was palpable in the rear vampire's rising tone.

"The master may be appeased," the leader muttered, "if we bring Cabot to him."

"But how? The bastard's gone."

"Not far. Look. There's a trail of blood..."

Leanna's head jerked up as the vampires approached. She fed the glamour, strengthening the shielding with all her magic. Legrand's minions drew up short, not three steps from their hiding place.

"The blood stops here. Completely."

The leader made a sound of frustration. "What foul magic is this? Damn Cabot. He's slipperier than an eel."

The trio lingered, trading opinions and curses. Eventually, they moved off. Several minutes passed before Leanna dared speak.

"They're gone."

Jackson didn't answer. He shifted away from her, until their bodies were no longer touching. Cautiously, Leanna sparked a glow of elflight within the protection of the glamour.

Jackson sat with his back against the cave wall, his forearms resting on his bent knees. Just above his bowed head, a corpse lay in its tomb. The linen strips binding its skeleton had begun to unravel.

When she met his gaze, what she saw in his eyes wasn't human, but vampire. Her heart stuttered.

Hunger. Stark, raw hunger.

His lips drew back in a snarl, exposing his fangs. She couldn't look away from his gleaming incisors. Couldn't help longing to feel them on her skin. Was it his vampire mesmerism causing the sudden flood of heat between her legs? Or was her own craving for death magic to blame?

"Jackson." She swallowed. "What's wrong? What's happening to you? To me?"

His voice was a low rasp. "I warned you to escape while you could. You didn't listen. Being this close to you...here in the darkness...with thirst clawing at my throat..." He swallowed, thickly. "Your blood. I can smell it, Leanna. Did you know that? The scent of it is so sweet..."

His exhale was a harsh moan. "Only the thinnest thread of humanity prevents me from sinking my fangs into your sweet neck and draining every last drop of blood from your body. Leave me, Leanna. Flee into the sun. Now, before it's too late."

"No."

The word was on her lips before she even willed it. Even so, she didn't regret it. "I won't go, Jackson. Don't ask me. I'm here for you."

She laid her hand on his chest. His heartbeat was so faint she couldn't feel it. "You don't have to steal my blood. I'm more than willing to give it to you."

"Why debase yourself? I have nothing to offer you but death magic. Obsession. Destruction. You don't want that, Leanna."

"I know what death magic is," Leanna said quietly. "I've practiced death magic. I summoned a powerful demon. In my arrogance, I thought I could bend it to my will. Instead, I became its slave. My soul is already tainted. A vampire's bite could hardly make it blacker. My blood is yours, Jackson. Take it. Please."

"Leanna—"

He gripped her head between his palms, roughly, and forced her to look at him. What she saw in his eyes made her mouth go dry. Jackson looked like the creature of death that he was. Ravenous. Unforgiving. How could the man she'd once known live behind those dead, burning eyes?

Somehow, she believed he did still live. He had to. She would not accept anything less. She forced herself to speak.

"I love you, Jackson. I always have and I always will. There's nothing you could do, nothing you could be, that would change that."

He closed his eyes, his expression pained. Leanna felt his bloodlust drain away.

"Damn it, Leanna. Do you know how many humans I've killed? How many innocents I've turned into undead monsters?"

"No. And I don't want to know. Don't tell me. It doesn't matter. I know who you are."

"Do you? Then you know more than I do."

She touched his cheek. So pale. Tears crowded her eyes. She reached for the man he once had been.

"Do you remember the evening we met?"

He closed his eyes briefly, but she didn't miss the flicker of humanity he tried to hide. "How could I not remember? You were standing at the bottom of the stair. I was coming out of the ballroom. You were surrounded by men, but I did not think you saw any of them. You looked...lost."

"No one else noticed how unhappy I was that night. No one cared what I was feeling. Especially not the artists hanging on my every word. They were too busy lusting after my magic. And ogling my bust."

"All I wanted was to make you laugh."

Leanna smiled. "And you did."

A reluctant amusement softened his features. "Toppling a waiter carrying a full tray of wineglasses wasn't part of any grand plan to provide for your amusement, I assure you."

"But when the merlot spilled into Mrs. Emerson's cleavage—"

Jackson chuckled. Leanna's heart leapt at the sound. "I thanked God and Heaven she didn't recognize me," he said. "She would have written my father. He would have demanded I cease my foolishness and return to Boston at once."

As quickly as Leanna's elation had risen, it fled. Her chest went hollow. "You never did go home. Because of me."

His smile faded. "Because I fell in love with you. I wanted to stay by your side. Make you laugh for as long as you wanted."

"A part of me wanted that, too. I loved you so very much."

"Did you really, Leanna? For a time I thought that might be true. During that long summer, every time I made you laugh. Every time we made love. And especially that night I painted your portrait."

Gods. Her portrait.

He paused, his throat working. "That painting is here in Rome. It hangs in the *Galleria Nazionale*. Did you know?"

"No, I didn't," Leanna said quietly. "But I'm not surprised. It was a true masterpiece."

"But it wasn't my masterpiece. It was your magic that created that portrait."

"It was what you came to Paris for, wasn't it? To create a work of great genius?"

"Initially, it was, until Paris showed me that what I thought was my great talent was in reality nothing more than the dabbling of a dilettante. But then I met you, and it didn't matter. All I wanted was your love."

"My love wasn't the prize you thought it was," Leanna said sadly. "My feelings for you—they were too frightening. I couldn't quite make myself believe you weren't lusting after the inspiration my magic could provide. I forced myself to treat you as I did the others. That night, I told myself that if you accepted my magic, if you used it to paint a masterpiece, it meant you didn't truly love me." She paused. "And you did paint that masterpiece, Jackson. I had never felt so betrayed as I did that night."

He stared at her, aghast. "That is why you left me? Because I took your muse magic?"

She nodded.

"Ah, Leanna. If only I had known, I would have burned every blank canvas I possessed."

"I'm not sure even that would have convinced me. No man had ever wanted me for myself. Only for my magic, and my body. Even my own father..." She blinked back hot, shameful tears. "I couldn't imagine anything different."

Jackson shut his eyes and did not answer. His breathing had roughened, she noted with some alarm. And his hands—they were shaking. His face had gone white as chalk. When he opened his eyes, it was clear his vision had lost its focus.

"You're getting weaker," Leanna said, dread curdling in her stomach. "You need blood. Take mine, Jackson. Please."

He wet his lips with his tongue. "Don't...don't tempt me."

"Why not? There's no danger. Sidhe can't turn vampire."

"But they can die. I thirst...so strongly. I could suck you dry in an instant."

She shifted so she was kneeling in front of him, and took his hands in hers. "You won't. I trust you."

His hands found her waist, his fingers flexing. "You shouldn't, Leanna. God knows I don't trust myself."

"Then I'll trust enough for both of us."

He tensed—she thought he would push her away. Then his fingers bit into her flesh.

She leaned into his embrace and brushed her lips across his. "Jackson..."

"Leanna, don't."

She ignored his plea. Opening her mouth, she ran her tongue along the seam of his lips. When she licked the point of his fang a profound shudder washed through him.

With a surrendering moan, he dragged her into his lap. Her arms encircled his neck. She pressed her body flush against his, her breasts squashed against his chest, her legs straddling his thighs. He was cold, so cold. She wanted more than anything to give him all the fire, all the life, in her soul.

His kisses sent drugging pleasure into her veins. Vampire magic? Or was she addicted to the man himself? His hands roamed her body, molding her breasts, cupping her arse, dragging up the hem of her dress. She felt his cool palm on the heated skin of her inner thigh.

She kissed a fervent line along his jaw, then scraped her cheek against his stubbled chin, stretching her neck, making herself vulnerable. He inhaled sharply as the point of his incisors scraped her throat's pulse. His erection pressed, hard and insistent, against her hip. A wave of aching lust took her breath. Her blood coursed in her veins, for him. Only for him.

The wanting cut like a knife. It sliced at her soul, carving it into thousands upon thousands of yearning pieces. And more. It was as if Jackson had released every atom from her body, allowing them to float free into the atmosphere. And then had recaptured and enslaved every particle of her being.

He cursed, his voice hoarse. "Leanna. You don't want this."

Not want it? At that moment, she would have willingly died for his bite. She gasped a sound that was half-laugh, half-moan.

"Gods, Jackson, I want you more than I want my next breath. Do it, Jackson. For you. For me."

For a long, heart-stopping moment, she thought he'd master his need of her. Perhaps it was a sign of how much the battle with Xaviere had cost him that his resistance lasted only a few heartbeats. Then his big body shook. She felt the damp of tears on her cheek.

She laid her hand on his head, threading her fingers through his hair.

He kissed her neck.

"Leanna."

He exhaled her name, his voice slipping into dark bliss. His body sank into his bite. It stung, but the pain was gone almost before she'd felt it.

The pull of her lips on her neck roused a shifting, writhing emotion in her heart. He seated his fangs more deeply into her flesh. Her response was a tide of sensation, unlike anything she'd ever known.

Pleasure. She'd expected that, of course. If vampires weren't masters of pleasure, humans wouldn't sell their souls for the privilege of submitting to undead fangs. The bliss was intense, but not unmanageable. She knew pleasure. She'd had it in so many ways, for so many years, from so many men, in light and in darkness.

But pleasure was only the beginning.

There was fear, too. A building sense of panic that somehow only augmented the erotic suction of Jackson's bite. Fear for her life, as blood pumped from her heart into his body. She felt as though her soul was traveling with it.

She couldn't move. Like a plump fly caught in a spider's silk, she was paralyzed. He could see into her soul, into her mind, into her darkest desires. She was vulnerable to whatever he chose to take from her. Or to give.

But she could not see into his soul, his mind, his desire.

The one-sided intimacy he forced on her was nearly unbearable. Leanna was skilled in hiding the essential aspects of her soul. She was used to separating her mind from her body when her emotions became too intense to face. She'd learned the technique as a girl just entering womanhood. It was the only way to endure her human father's hands on her body.

For years, even after she'd come into the fullness of her Sidhe power and fled the Highlands, her sordid adolescence had colored every interaction she'd had with men. She'd never revealed her true soul to her lovers. She'd always remained hidden.

But now, with Jackson, she couldn't hide. He'd stripped her bare, laid out her soul in the sunlight for his leisurely perusal and his complete possession. Jackson's vampire bite did more than touch her soul. It shredded it. Inhaled it. Consumed it.

And all she could do was accept it.

The bite seemed to stretch on and on, pleasure and pain spinning into eternity. She felt her blood flowing into him. It was an exquisite sensation. If he lost control, if he drained her, she wouldn't even protest. When he pulled back at last, she cried out and tried to prevent him from leaving her.

The room swayed. She'd lost her hold on the elflight, and the spell had begun to flash like a strobe. Jackson's handsome face flickered in and out of darkness. His fangs, tinged with her blood, glinted. She licked her own lips, almost expecting to taste it.

His eyes focused on the slight movement, going dark and darker still. They were now so black she thought she might plunge into their velvet depths and never emerge.

His lids lowered. Finally, she managed to draw a breath. Then he bent his head, his lips again seeking her neck.

She arched to receive him. But the sting didn't come. His tongue flicked gently over her wound, the only sensation a pleasant tingle. The lingering pain of the puncture disappeared. When she brought her fingers to her neck, she felt only unbroken skin.

His tone was self-mocking. "This is when I usually wipe a victim's memory along with her wound. I could do the same to you, if you'd like."

"No," Leanna whispered, blushing. A part of her desperately wanted to erase those agonizing seconds of raw vulnerability, but the thought of Jackson remembering, while she forgot, was too much to bear. "No, please don't."

He nodded and stood, propping one shoulder against a solid section of wall between two tiers of tombs, his back half-turned to her. Leanna drew her legs up to her chest, hugging them. Watching him. As the seconds ticked by, she became more aware of her body. Oddly, she didn't feel dirty and drained, as a vampire's victim usually did after a bite. Instead she felt...clean. Calm.

Almost peaceful.

"Did...did you take enough? I thought you might have...stopped too quickly."

He glanced down at her and then away.

"I took what I needed. You have Sidhe blood, after all."

From his tone, she couldn't tell if that was a good thing. Slowly, she stood.

"Is Sidhe blood a problem?"

"Far from it. Your blood is much more alive than a full human's." He exhaled and turned, pressing his shoulder blades flat against the cave wall. "That sip from your veins...I think it replaced most of what I'd hoarded before we..."

She blushed. "I'm glad." A thought occurred to her. "Will another sip make you even stronger? Strong enough to destroy Legrand? I'll...I'm willing to give you more of my blood, Jackson. Whatever you need."

"No, Leanna."

The finality of his tone chilled her to the bone. "But—"

"You won't give me anything more. Not blood, not comfort, not aid." He dragged a hand over his face and she realized he was shaking. He gestured toward his groin. Leanna took in the size of the bulge in his pants and drew a sharp breath.

He laughed, crudely. "Do you honestly think I could drink more from your sweet neck without ripping that pitiful scrap of a dress right off your body? Without wrenching your thighs open and plunging inside? Without pounding myself inside you, using you, defiling you, until long after you scream for me to stop?"

The raw erotic images his word painted in her mind nearly buckled her knees. She couldn't seem to gasp enough air.

"I wouldn't beg for you to stop, Jackson. I'd beg for you to make it last forever."

His lips pressed together briefly, as if in pain. When he spoke, his eyes were flat and dead, and his voice was low. His words vibrated with ruthless resolve.

"You don't know what you're saying. You don't know what it would mean, being chained to me for eternity. That is, if you even survived the full force of my lust. You cannot imagine how close I am to losing all control. That is why you are going to turn around and walk into the light. You will climb into the sun and you will not look back."

"No, I won't do it. I—"

"I don't need you any longer. Leanna. And I don't want you, either."

His words hurt. She told herself that they were lies, that he was protecting her the only way he knew. Somehow, that didn't make the pain of his rejection any easier to bear.

"If I go, what will you do?"

He didn't answer.

"You're going to confront Legrand, aren't you? You're going to challenge Europe's master. Tonight, as soon as the sun sets, even though you know you're not sure you're strong enough to win. And you won't take more of my blood, when you know it would give you the advantage."

"Leanna...don't. I feel my strength returning...Perhaps I'm even stronger than before I came to your hotel room. I believe I have a chance to defeat Legrand tonight. Leave, Leanna. You've given me what I need."

"It's not enough. Jackson, don't turn me away now. I want to help you."

"You've helped me enough already." His eyes seemed to soften.

"I want to help more! Just hours ago, you were ready to force me to fight Legrand for you."

"That was before I realized I—" Abruptly, he crossed his arms. "That was before, when I was angry. My rage seems to have burned itself out. Now, I want only for you to leave me. Now, Leanna. I won't have your life on my conscience."

"That's your pride speaking."

"Pride?" He laughed. "Hardly. I lost whatever pride I once had long ago. Guilt, perhaps? Now that, I admit, I have in abundance." A shadow crossed his features. "Solange—she was above ground, guarding my lair. Now she's been taken, as Jean-Claude was." His shoulders slumped. "I've failed both of them. I won't rest until I free them from Legrand's clutches."

"Which is exactly why you need my help! What good will it do if you die trying to rescue them?"

Chapter Eleven

Not six months earlier, Leanna had sworn on the silver branches of Annwyn's eternal tree of life that she would never kill again.

Ah, well, she'd known the chances of her keeping that sacred oath were slim. Still, she hadn't expected she'd abandon the vow quite so soon, nor quite so spectacularly. So far, she'd killed three of Legrand's human stewards, as well as his most powerful deputy.

Xaviere had been a monster. It had felt good to destroy him. She repressed a shudder. What did that say about her soul? Nothing good, she was sure, but at the moment, she wasn't willing to stop and do any soul-searching. Not when there was more killing to accomplish.

She hadn't wanted to leave Jackson, but he'd given her no choice in the matter. The sun had been high when she emerged from the catacombs, dragging her dust-covered suitcase with her. It had taken her eyes a good hour to adapt to the light.

She'd checked into a room at a cheap *pensione* to prepare. Now it was late afternoon. Long shadows crept over the warren of medieval buildings of Rome's historic center. Emerging from a twisting alley into a blaze of artificial light, Leanna paused. Piazza Navona buzzed with activity—mimes and magicians, café chatter, peddlers hawking trinkets. The club outfit Solange had stashed in Leanna's bag showed quite a lot of skin, but no one gave her more than a cursory glance. Vampire sluts were a common enough sight in the city.

Careful of her spiked heels on the uneven cobbles, Leanna picked her way across the piazza to stand beside its central fountain. Maybe the life magic of the cascading water would soothe her rising anxiety.

It didn't.

Clasping her clutch bag to her stomach, she stared at the sculptures ringing fountain. She'd been here just a week ago, with Kalen and Christine. That innocent tourist outing seemed like it had happened a lifetime ago to an entirely different woman.

The nearest sculpture showed a man lying on his side, one arm upraised as if shielding his eyes from an unspeakable horror. Above him rose the beautiful façade of a baroque church. Kalen, ever the art aficionado, had explained to Christine and Leanna that the church's architect had been a bitter rival of the fountain's sculptor. The sculptor had carved the cringing figure to mock his adversary. At the time, Leanna had barely given the story a thought. Now, the long-dead artist's contempt for his enemy, frozen in stone for eternity, chilled her to the bone.

Hate could last so very, very long.

She thought of her last glimpse of Jackson, before she'd finally obeyed him, turning and climbing out of the catacombs without a backward glance. His eyes had been flat, his jaw rigid. He wouldn't accept her help. He didn't want her blood. He'd closed his mind and his heart to her. His entire being had been focused on his hatred of Legrand.

Yes, hate endured, long after love was gone.

The last rays of the setting sun burnished the piazza's stuccoed buildings to rich amber, then to deep chocolate. As daylight faded, Leanna left the fountain. Slipping around a large group of German tourists, she made her way to an alley at the far end of the piazza.

The passage existed in gloom. Canyon-like walls loomed high on either side. The buzz of the crowd faded as she moved farther into the shadows. After several twists and turns she halted before a doorway framed by a chiseled stone arch. The entrance was unexceptional and bore no sign other than the number "6" etched on a brass plate. The door knocker was fashioned in the shape of a cat's head. The eyes were ruby-red stones, glowing faintly.

For the hundredth time, she wondered if she was doing the right thing entering this place alone. The wise thing to have done was return to her posh hotel, or at least try to call Mac on her cell phone, which she'd found in her luggage. She did neither, though she had stashed the phone in her purse. She was aware of its weight, taunting her.

Her decision not to go to Mac for help weighed on her conscience, but she was sure she'd done the right thing in keeping him out of it. Yes, she'd told Jackson that Mac would help him, but the notion had been a fantasy. Once bathed in the light of day, she faced reality. Mac was a light magic demigod. He despised vampires. He wanted nothing to do with their dealings and gave their meeting places a wide berth.

Jackson was perfectly right in believing Mac wouldn't exactly jump at the chance to enter Legrand's lair and stake the vampire master as a favor to a vampire who'd kidnapped his sister. Quite the contrary—she was certain Mac would do everything in his power to prevent Leanna from doing the job on her own. She couldn't allow that. Better that Mac believe she was lounging at a Tuscan spa until the deed was done.

She executed a meticulous scan of her glamour magic even though she'd checked it not five minutes earlier. And five minutes before that. To fool Legrand, the glamour had to be perfect, hiding her Sidhe magic as well as changing her appearance. He'd be suspicious of any Sidhe voluntarily seeking out a vampire. Worse, he might recognize her as the Celtic *leannan-sidhe* muse who'd once blazed a path through the Parisian demimonde.

She drew a deep breath. No sense in stalling on the threshold of her goal. She lifted the knocker and let it fall. A thud reverberated in the hollow space beyond.

Mere heartbeats later, the door opened.

The spidery-looking doorman was vampire, recently turned. The youth's jerking, mechanical movements coupled with the wild panic in his eyes told the sordid story. His features were twisted with equal parts hopelessness and revulsion. He was a slave. No—less than a slave. A slave at least had the hope of escape. A newly made vampire did not.

Leanna struggled to imagine Jackson in the pathetic youth's place. She couldn't. Even flat on his back, drained and wounded, Jackson exuded power. Raw, angry magic. A force that Leanna could almost believe had a chance against Legrand's endless evil.

But she wouldn't take the chance that he might fail.

She crossed over the threshold and brushed past the doorman. He made no protest. She entered a long, dark hallway that narrowed like a funnel. It ended at a linen-draped table. The pallid female vampire sitting behind it flicked undead eyes over Leanna.

Leanna knew what the vampire saw: a stunning human female, tall and blonde, with long, lithe legs and breasts large enough to suffocate a man. Those breasts were trussed into a black lace corset that left little to the imagination. A wisp of a black miniskirt—with nothing beneath—barely covered a lush round arse. Silver chains dangled from lace garters, clipped to the sheerest of black silk stockings. The five-inch wooden stilettos she wore were sharp enough to impale. It was a testament to Legrand's strength that his door attendant didn't seem concerned.

"One hundred Euros. Cash," was all she said.

Leanna snapped open her clutch and extracted the notes. The vamp snatched the money and, with a jerk of her head, indicated a solid black door.

The doorknob was hot. Leanna's heart pounded as she stepped through the door and closed it behind her. She found herself on the edge of a crowded dance floor, in a room that was almost as dark as Jackson's catacomb. Death metal vomited from hidden speakers, so loud it seemed as though it had erupted inside Leanna's skull.

Her heart skipped a beat in an effort to match the aberrant rhythm. The notes were laced with death magic, strong enough to make Leanna's blood vibrate. Writhing bodies crammed the dance floor. Human throats stretched for their undead partners. She looked away as an ancient vamp sunk rotting fangs into a teenage girl's neck.

She advanced a few steps, her eyes adjusting to the thick, smoky atmosphere, barely brightened by anemic wall sconces. Someone shoved a glass in her hand. The metallic odor of its contents caused her stomach to spasm. Blood. She looked up to find a pale vamp watching her, his lip stained red. When she caught his gaze, he lifted his glass to her. His lips drew back, exposing his fangs.

She felt her gorge rise.

Turning abruptly, she threaded her way through the crowd, pressing her full glass into the first pair of empty hands she saw. The edges of the room were dark, and darker still where the main space faded into semi-private alcoves. Human shadows wrestled and pulsed in the niches, amid sighs and groans of rancid pleasure.

The erotic symphony disgusted Leanna. The dance room was a waste of her time. She knew how vamp clubs operated—the owners rarely mingled with riff-raff off the street. Legrand would be ensconced in a private parlor, entertaining victims hand-picked by his most trusted minions. She noted a handful of those elite guards pacing the perimeter of the dance floor, silently watching.

A stair in the corner of the room led to rooms on the upper levels, where humans and vamps could exchange sex along with blood. Leanna considered the possibility that Legrand was in one of those rooms, then almost as quickly rejected the notion. A vampire as ancient as he would not tolerate a berth above ground. The master would be below.

Should she approach one of his minions and offer herself for his master's pleasure? It was all too likely one of the brutes would try to keep her for himself. No, better if she employed a bit of Sidhe stealth and searched for Legrand on her own terms.

She spotted a staircase nestled in an alcove behind the bar, spiraling downward. Two vampires stood guard. One male, one female. They were fairly old, but for all the power bristling around them, they were hardly on their most alert behavior. In fact, they looked extremely bored.

Good.

It was easy enough to enhance her glamour with a look-away spell that made her nearly invisible. It was harder, however, to move through the crowd undetected—the club's patrons were packed tight, thigh to chest. Leanna made slow progress toward the stair.

Eventually, she reached the sentinels. Neither the male nor the female glanced her way as she slipped past. Still, Leanna could not suppress a sigh of relief as she rounded the stair's first curve.

The circling steps seemed to go on forever. Finally, the flight ended in a short corridor blocked by a heavy, iron-strapped door. The look must have been mainly for effect, because the lock was a mundane mortise affair. A concentrated blast of elfshot dissolved it quite easily. Behind the door, the twisted descent of yet another stair gave out to a parlor of sorts. The carpet was lush, the furniture upholstered in leather. The walls were bare and ancient. The cellar was a Roman-era ruin, its diamond-shaped stone bricks forming a pattern reminiscent of a fisherman's net. The space seemed to be deserted, but the air of menace was unmistakable.

Cool dampness chilled the bare skin above Leanna's stockings and raised goose bumps on her arms and the back of her neck. She tried her best to ignore the sensation of being lured into a snare.

A single exit pierced the opposite wall. A horizontal slash of light shone beneath it. As Leanna approached, she became aware of sounds slithering beneath the portal. The whistle and crack of a whip, a man's sharp cry, a guttural groan, a sign of bliss. Her stomach turned. She swallowed the bile in her throat and put her hand on the doorframe.

This door sported an iron latch and a single old-fashioned keyhole. Kneeling, she pressed her eye to the hole. What she saw in that narrow field of vision caused her gorge to rise anew.

Leanna had been a slave in the demon realms, had even descended into the pit of Hell itself. She'd seen things, awful things that haunted her dreams still. But this? This somehow was worse. Because she knew what she was witnessing had been Jackson's fate long ago. A fate to which Leanna had delivered him.

She wanted to run. Instead, she summoned every ounce of her once-famous audacity and lifted the latch. The door opened easily. She strode boldly into the light of a hundred dancing candles.

The illumination was unwelcome. If the dungeon room had been dark, the massive width of Legrand's bare shoulders, flexing as he whipped a naked youth manacled to an X-shaped wooden frame, would have been nothing more than a shadow. In deeper gloom, the angry stripes crisscrossing the victim's shoulders and back, and the blood smeared over his buttocks would have been invisible. But even in the dark Leanna would have heard the whistle of the metal-tipped flogger, and the sharp, agonized cry of the vampire master's victim.

Could the youth be Jackson's unfortunate steward, Jean-Claude? She became certain her guess was correct when her gaze touched on a velvet chaise where an unconscious woman lay. Solange. Her neck was exposed, but unmarred. Her face, though pale, wasn't dulled by the death tinge of a newly made vampire. She was still among the living, for the moment, at least. Leanna let out a slow breath. It came out louder than she'd intended.

Legrand paused in his flogging, his head cocked. Slowly, he turned. For a moment he assessed the newcomer, saying nothing. His bloody whip dangling from his long fingers as his eyes roamed her body.

Leanna lifted her chin, thrust out her chest, and met the vampire's gaze with silent, provocative challenge. Inside her fears churned. Europe's vampire master was a large man, close to seven feet tall. His massive chest and arms, bared to view, bulged with muscle. Legrand had been in his prime when he'd died. Two millennia had done little to mar his physical perfection.

He brought his whip hand to his face and shoved a hank of black hair from his eyes. Sweat shone on his forehead; his leather pants—his only garment—hung undone, crudely revealing yet another physical endowment that fit his grandiose name.

The scent of sexual ecstasy, extracted from his suffering victim, clung to him like dung. A low, wretched sound spilled from the young man's lips. A determined chill stiffened Leanna's spine. Legrand was truly a monster. This undead aberration must be destroyed.

Casually, she laid her evening bag on a low table.

"Ah. What have we here?" Legrand's nimble tongue flicked over bloodstained lips. His eyes raked her body, sending a sensation like a scurry of insect legs across her skin. For one heart-stopping instant, she feared he'd seen through her glamour. But no, he was only assessing his latest plaything.

"My minions have sent a delicious new morsel." The vampire's accent carried a hint of the aristocratic; his features, Leanna thought, had once been handsome.

"So they have," she murmured.

"They are well accustomed to anticipating their master's needs." Legrand flicked his whip toward his bound slave, opening a new slash and raising a hiss from the man's throat. "I grow bored with this one. He will be much more amusing when my newest slave recovers from the blow she took to her head." His smiling gaze traveled to Solange. "Do you know, my sweet, this woman was once wed to my newest pet? When she wakes, I'll have my fill of her while he watches. Then I'll instruct him to drain her veins."

Jean-Claude strained against his bonds, eyes blazing with helpless fury. "Damn you to Hell, Legrand."

The vampire spun and landed a vicious blow to Jean-Claude's torn and bloody skin. The prisoner's spine arched, a cry choking in his throat. On the second blow, he went slack and silent. His head lolled to one side.

"Finally, peace. Ah, well, this one is young and stubborn. It will take some time yet to break him. Until then…" Legrand smiled, showing his fangs. "New blood as sweet as yours is always welcome."

It took all Leanna's self-control to keep her revulsion from showing on her face.

Legrand's gaze crawled down her body. "My minions should have instructed you to strip before you approached me. Do it now, and be quick about it."

Leanna froze.

Legrand's eyes narrowed. His grip shifted on the whip handle.

Leanna forced her shaking hands to the top hook of her corset. There was no hope of resisting Legrand's command. This was what she'd come for, after all. The quicker begun, the quicker done. She popped open the top hook. Her breasts strained. Legrand's gaze slithered to her cleavage.

"Very nice," he murmured. "Go on."

She dropped her arms to her sides and took one careful step toward him. "But..." she protested in silky French. "That would be so...ordinary. Surely you don't wish to take me as you do your other...lovers."

He seemed amused. "And why not? In almost a thousand years of existence, I've learned my own desires."

She moved closer, on silent feet, until she stood less than an arm's length away from the monster. "Give me a chance to prove I can give you something new. Something...unique. I came to Rome only for you, after all."

"That is nothing new. Many seek me out."

"None of them are like me."

She was taking a grave risk, but she had to chance it. Legrand was even more brutal, more depraved than she'd imagined. She could feel his power humming, reaching for her. If she wanted to throw him off-balance, she had to capture his curiosity. Now. But she was well aware of the fine line she walked. She must not reveal too much.

She inhaled, thrusting her breasts forward as she lifted her arms and smoothed her hair back from her face. She let her glamour drop, just a little. Enough to reveal delicate, pointed ears.

The vampire's surprise was evident. "But what is this? A Sidhe?"

"No, I'm human. Mostly. But I have a little Sidhe blood. Enough to interest you, I hope." Leanna tensed, waiting for Legrand to see through her ruse.

He reached out, grasping her chin in his fingers. She tried not to gasp. He smiled indulgently. She forced herself to relax. Thank the gods, he didn't seem to recognize how dangerous she was.

"Your life essence is very strong," he said.

"I will give it to you. Gladly. For a taste of your death magic."

He released her chin and moved his hand to her neck. He wrapped his fingers around the slender column and flexed with gentle menace.

"What game do you play? The Sidhe abhor death magic."

Leanna's pulse beat against his thumb. "But humans do not. My human desires far overwhelm my Sidhe nature. Here," she whispered. "I'll show you."

Before she could change her mind, she opened her soul. Digging deep, she touched the dark stain on her life essence that would never be completely cleansed, not even if she lived in Annwyn for a thousand years. Red lights spun in her vision; her head grew light. She nearly gagged at the foulness of what she'd been, of what she'd done in her past. Choking back revulsion, she brought her eternal shame forward and let it seep into Legrand's mind.

His smile spread as the filth of what she'd once been washed through him. His brows rose. A greedy gleam leaped into his eyes.

He licked his lips. "You are a demonwhore."

"I was. No more. My masters met defeat at the hands of their enemies and I escaped the death realms. Since then I've tried to erase the death magic from my soul, but I found...that isn't possible. Death is part of me. I think of it, I dream of it. I crave it."

Shameful heat crept up her neck. Her words were not the lies she wished they were.

"And so," she whispered, "I've come to you. Death's master. My master."

"My slave." His gaze, his touch, his breath—they were grimy fingers picking over her body, her mind, her soul. He smiled, showing large teeth, slightly yellowed, stained around the edges with fresh blood.

The mesmerizing touch of his mind slid into her brain. She didn't resist—couldn't resist—as he walked backward. The backs of her knees bumped a cushioned surface. An armchair. She sat. Legrand loomed large above her, his muscular legs spreading her thighs. Leaning forward, he released a foul tide of dark magic. It burned every inch of her skin.

"Lift your arms over your head."

She obeyed without hesitation. Indeed, there was no way to resist. His magic was strong; far stronger, she realized, than Jackson's. Had Jackson truly believed he could destroy Legrand? Leanna knew that he could not.

But she could. At the moment Legrand climaxed inside her, she would release her muse magic and drain every last drop of stolen life essence from his damned soul. The thought of taking him inside her body, where Jackson had so recently been, left a bitter residue in her throat. She swallowed hard and tried to expand her tightening ribs.

She was terrified. But her fear for herself, for what she was about to do, was nothing compared to her fear for Jackson. Jackson was strong, but Legrand was stronger. A battle between the two could only end in Jackson's obliteration. She would not allow that to happen.

His hands were on her. His sharp fingernails scraped painfully, shredding her corset to ribbons until it fell away, baring her breasts. He continued stroking. Dark pleasure trailed in lines of fire over her skin. It was false pleasure, she knew—a vampire's illusion. But it felt all too real. She gasped at the brazen intimacy of it and tried not to think of Jackson. He would not want to touch her ever again, once Legrand had defiled her. But that didn't matter, as long as Legrand was dead and Jackson was safe.

"Look at me," Legrand commanded.

She did. His eyes were dark, completely so. No variation showed between iris and pupil. The orbs shone with deadly light. Leanna wished with all her heart that she could summon the strength to look away.

A fingernail traced up the inside of her leg, pausing high on her inner thigh. "You were not lying when you promised uniqueness. I can smell your blood. It is sweeter than anything I have known. And I have known much."

He went down on his knees and yanked off her shoes. Ripped her stockings. She tensed as he bent his head over her foot, teeth scraping each of her toes in turn. His tongue, like flame, licked at her soles.

Leanna felt a pinch, felt him lick away a drop of her life essence. Drugging weakness weighted her limbs. He didn't seem to be in any hurry to have sex. She wanted to move, to encourage him, but her limbs would not obey. Trapped like a puppet on his string, she spun slowly, slowly, panic welling. Darkness rushed her brain; adrenaline alone kept her from losing consciousness. Gods. Did Legrand want her senseless before he used her? If she succumbed to this drugging fog, she wouldn't be able to cast her magic.

"Sweet," he mused. "So sweet."

His breath was hot on the arch of her foot. Was he contemplating another nip? How long would he toy with her before he sank his fangs into her pulse and drank deeply? How much could she endure before blacking out?

She would not let him win this encounter. She managed to angle her head just enough to catch his gaze. His brows raised.

"Come inside me," she whispered.

He showed his fangs. "Patience, my pet."

"No. I can't wait." She begged him like the whore she'd once been. "I'll go mad if you don't take me now."

"Madness has its own pleasures. You may find you prefer it to sanity."

"Please. I need you..."

He stroked her calf. Death magic emanated from the pores of his fingers. Foul. Familiar. Once she had gloried in the sensation. Now it inspired only revulsion. What she'd felt when she'd made love with Jackson had been nothing like this. Her fears had been unfounded, she realized now. With Jackson, it hadn't been death magic at all. It had been love.

His strokes lengthened, creeping up her thigh. Her gorge rose, her vision went black around the edges. It was all she could do to keep the rolling darkness at bay.

"Inside me," she groaned. "Now. Please."

Legrand's hands left her. He stood, looking down at her in the chair. His gaze was fixed on the pulse point of her neck; his magic was holding her motionless. She could barely breathe. If he chose to drain her blood before entering her body, her magic would be useless.

She waited, suspended on a knife's edge of terror. His hands fell to his groin, stroking.

"As you wish, *mon cher*. Stand and remove what is left of your clothing."

She rose and put some distance between them. Her every instinct recoiled from his command, but she would not back down now. She prayed his climax, the moment she could release her muse magic, would not take long. She fixed her mind on the point in the very near future when Legrand would lay senseless, drained of his life essence. The instant he succumbed, she'd snatch up her shoe and drive the heel straight through his heart.

Her hands shook as she slid out of her skirt. It hit the floor, leaving her naked. Soon, she told herself. Soon. Legrand would lie at her feet, dead forever this time. His evil would never rise again.

It was a good plan. A brilliant plan.

It might even have worked.

If only Jackson Cabot hadn't chosen that precise moment to burst into his enemy's lair.

Chapter Twelve

The shock of seeing Jean-Claude strapped to Legrand's flogging frame was bad enough. The sight of Solange's pale, still body was even worse. But finding Leanna standing naked before Legrand…

Pure rage boiled in Jackson's veins, evaporating every rational thought. His vision bled red. In a flash, he propelled his body across the room. Leanna screamed as he flung her behind him.

"You idiot!" she spat.

He spun to face his adversary. Legrand took in Jackson's unexpected appearance with typical nonchalance. Straightening, he adjusted his cock and buttoned it back into his trousers.

"Cabot. *Quelle surprise.* Apparently, my minions have gone lax." He glanced at Leanna. "Was this one yours? You must have left her sorely dissatisfied or she would not have come to me."

Leanna shoved past Jackson, as if trying to protect him. Was the woman insane? Again, Jackson thrust her behind him.

"Jackson—"

"Shut up," he barked. "Stay back."

Legrand's lips curled in a smile. "No need to growl, Cabot. In fact, you're more than welcome to join us." He opened his arms wide, in a gesture that encompassed Jean-Claude and Solange. "Indeed, once your former stewards regain consciousness, all five of us could—"

"Bastard. You know why I'm here. It's time. I challenge you, Legrand. We fight. Here. Now. To the end."

"A duel, Cabot? Most unwise. You cannot defeat me."

"We shall see."

His lot was cast. He would win or die. Completely, this time. Revenge or oblivion would be his. He tried not to think of what his defeat would mean for the others in this dungeon. Failure here would haunt him in Hell for all eternity.

Legrand's eyes flashed bright with good humor as he strolled to the whipping frame. He stroked a slow hand across Jean-Claude's bloody buttocks. Jackson's stomach turned.

"How long has it been since I took this one from you? Two months? Three? You'll be pleased to know he fights with unceasing hatred. I am vastly entertained."

Legrand turned and paced to the chaise. Jackson's eyes followed him.

"This one will battle as ferociously, I am sure. She will struggle against my first bite and everything that comes after. But your Sidhe mongrel?" His eyes found Leanna. "She does not fight at all. She begs for my cock. I am surprised, Cabot. Such a minion is not in keeping with your usual standards."

Jackson's jaw set. "Nevertheless, she is mine."

"Ah, but that is where you are wrong. She belongs to me, body and soul. I will use both to the utmost." He paused, smiling. "After I destroy you."

Jackson flexed his fists. "There will be no 'after.' Not for you."

Legrand smiled. "We shall see."

***

Jackson and Legrand circled slowly, eyes locked, an aura of death rising between them. Leanna threw her Sidhe power into the churning magic, intent on bolstering Jackson's cause. Her spell slammed up against a psychic wall. She barely managed to duck the rebound.

"It's no use." A hoarse whisper intruded. Her head whipped around. She hadn't realized Jean-Claude had regained consciousness. He twisted his neck to look at her. "No one may interfere with two vampires dueling for dominance."

"But—there must be some way to help Jackson."

"No. I am sorry."

A squeal like fingernails on a blackboard snapped Leanna's attention back to the battle. Legrand, moving so quickly his body was no more than a blur, hurtled toward Jackson. The outline of Jackson's body fuzzed as he dodged. Legrand smashed into the ancient stone wall. The room reverberated with the shock of the impact.

Candleflame flickered wildly; one taper fell to the floor, smoldering. Leanna dashed over and beat it out with a quick spell.

Legrand sprang to his feet, growling. Blood streaked down his temple.

Jackson crouched at the ready. "Feeling your age, Legrand?"

Legrand snarled, the fingernails of his clenched hands lengthening into claws. His body blurred a second time. This time, his assault struck its mark. Leanna's lungs seized as Jackson and his foe collided, then fell in a heap onto the armchair. The chair's legs snapped. Rolling violently onto the floor, the combatants veered toward Solange. Jean-Claude cried out, desperately twisting to break free, then slumping in relief when the vampires narrowly missed smashing into the chaise where his wife lay.

Leanna dashed to Jean-Claude's side. It took several moments to fashion a spell to open the first manacle, but at last the lock gave way with a blessed click. He hissed as the iron sprang open, revealing a ring of macerated flesh. Grimly aware of the duel crashing behind her, Leanna worked the remaining shackles.

Jean-Claude's knees buckled as he stumbled free. Leanna tried to catch him, but his weight threw her off balance and they tumbled to the floor. He righted himself quickly, wincing as he rose into a crouch. His sharp eyes tracked the blur of movement in the center of the room. Waves of death energy radiated from the duel.

"Can you tell what's going on? Who's winning?"

Jean-Claude half-stumbled, half-crawled to his wife's side, positioning his battered body between Solange and the battling vampires. The deep whip cuts on his skin were starting to close.

"No," he said. "Jackson was eager to issue this challenge, but Solange and I..." He shot a glance toward his wife. "We feared he was not ready. We wanted him to wait another year, at least..."

Bending over Solange, he cupped her pale cheek.

"Solange. My love. Can you hear me?"

There was no response.

The battling vampires crashed into the flogging frame. The heavy piece skidded across the floor and exploded against the wall, splintering into a hundred pieces. Leanna ducked behind Solange's chaise as debris showered over her. A smoking candle struck the upholstery. Quickly, Leanna spoke a spell to extinguish the flame. Jean-Claude hunched his shoulders over his wife.

Leanna peered over the back of the chaise. Damn. Several more small fires smoldered, smoke seeping into the air. "This can't go on much longer. There must be some way to help Jackson."

"There is not. It will be a fight to the death." Jean-Claude lifted Solange into his arms. "We should flee."

"Run away? Are you insane? We can't just abandon him!"

"Jackson would command it, if he could," he said. But reluctance shadowed his eyes. "If Jackson wins the duel, he will rule Europe and all will be well. If he loses..." His arms flexed around his wife's limp body. "Solange needs care. A head start will increase her chance of survival."

Leanna could only nod. "I understand. Go. Take her to safety. I'm staying."

"But there is nothing you can do here."

"I can't accept that. I have magic. Strong magic. There must be some way I can help Jackson."

Jean-Claude met her gaze for a long moment, then nodded. He turned toward the door without another word. Standing very still, Leanna stared into the shimmering energy at the center of the room. If only she could tell who was winning. Frustrated, she shot a blast of elfshot over the battle. The bolt ricocheted around the room like trapped lightning.

As the blurred movement of the sizzling green fire dissipated, the haze in the center of the room cleared. Legrand, bloody and battered, stood amid the smoke and detritus of his ruined dungeon. He bulging forearm was clamped around Jackson's neck from behind, pinning him to his chest. Jackson was struggling to free himself, to no avail. Leanna's heart sank as the man she loved surrendered to the vampire master's greater strength.

Jackson's body sagged like a rag doll. His eyes glazed, but did not close.

"Gods, no," Leanna whispered.

Legrand showed his fangs. "Should I snap his neck now?" He seemed to consider. "But no, that is too merciful. There is a more pleasant way to destroy a traitor."

With a dark laugh, Legrand heaved Jackson into the air. He hit the wall, skull cracking against the stone in an impact that would have killed a living man. Jackson slid to the floor, eyes blank, head lolling.

Rage, pure and raw, rose in Leanna's throat. She thought she screamed; she couldn't be sure. The surge of her magic blotted out her mundane senses. Raising both hands, she flung a double blast of elfshot at Legrand's head.

The vampire met the assault with one upraised hand, absorbing the green sparks into his palm with practiced ease. His fangs flashed a sneer. Leanna found herself stumbling backward, her brain once again captive to the vampire master's will. The back of her knees hit the chaise. She stumbled and fell. Out of the corner of her eye, she saw Jean-Claude clawing at the dungeon door, Solange's body slumped against the wall beside him. The oak slab didn't budge; its hinges and latch were fused shut. Leanna realized with horror that her own errant elfshot had melted the iron.

"On your feet," Legrand barked at Leanna.

Leanna's limbs lurched. Calmly, Legrand bent and retrieved a long shard of wood, a remnant of the flogging frame. Her fingers closed around it.

"I have decided," he said, "that you will destroy your erstwhile lover." He pressed the stake into Leanna's hand. "Lay Cabot on the floor. Then plunge this into his heart."

Leanna tried to force a refusal past her lips. They would not move. She tried to swallow. Her throat was paralyzed.

The rest of her body was not. Clutching the stake to her chest, she stumbled toward Jackson. His chest heaved; his dull eyes tracked her. He didn't resist as she set the stake on the ground and crouched to grab his ankles.

She dragged him away from the wall. The back of his head hit the ground. His limbs were limp, his body unmoving except for the harsh rise and fall of his chest. His eyes, however, were open and fully lucid. He knew what she was doing.

He knew that, once again, she was going to destroy him—completely, this time.

Blindly, propelled by a dark magic she couldn't begin to fight, Leanna picked up the stake. Legrand gave a grunt of satisfaction. He watched with avid good humor as she lurched to her feet and raised the splintered shaft high over her head. The jagged point was poised over Jackson's heart, suspended for the fatal blow.

Dark waves of magic swept over her. The urge to strike was overwhelming.

No! Leanna's mind screamed. *No!*

Her arms tensed; her shoulders flexed. This couldn't happen. She couldn't kill Jackson. Not again.

With gut-wrenching effort, Leanna reached for her strongest magic. It was hidden beneath the darkest part of her soul, behind a wounded, ugly place that frightened her so badly she couldn't bear to open it to the light. The ugly stain inside her meant she would never be whole, no matter how long she lived, no matter how hard she tried. The deepest part of herself bore permanent scars, inflicted by her Sidhe mother, her human father. By all the men who had ever used her for her magic. By her time in Hell. But the most painful wounds were the ones Leanna had inflicted on herself—those caused by her willing acts of dark magic.

But beneath the scars—behind the darkness and the hell she'd constructed for herself—ah, there a place of pure life survived. It was a place where risk was still possible. A place where love remained true.

The stake, driven by Legrand's will, whipped downward. Leanna grasped at the magic in that long forgotten, innocent corner of her soul. She had no time to form the power. No time to refine her intentions into a coherent spell. She could only fling the raw magic, messily, just as the stake pierced Jackson's flesh.

His torso jumped, as if shocked by live wires.

And then he lay still.

Horror tightened iron bands around Leanna's chest. She couldn't breathe, couldn't cry out. She could only stare at the stake she'd driven deep into Jackson's chest. She couldn't feel her fingers. They'd gone numb, clenched like claws around the splintered wood. She couldn't pry them loose, not even to escape the bubbling spurt of Jackson's blood.

She knelt motionless in the spreading crimson puddle. She'd failed.

Chapter Thirteen

Legrand threw back his head and laughed.

And laughed and laughed and laughed.

Leanna's world contracted until it was filled with nothing but that soulless mirth. Nothing but Legrand's handsome, twisted face. Nothing but his flat, evil eyes.

Nothing but her hands, ripping the bloody stake from Jackson's chest.

Nothing but her body, slowly pivoting.

Moving. Lunging.

Nothing but the blow she struck, straight into Legrand's heart.

Nothing but the flash of shocked comprehension in his eyes.

Nothing but his slow, open-mouthed fall to the ground.

Nothing but blood and death and bitter, bitter regret.

Chapter Fourteen

Leanna nearly fell onto Legrand's blood-soaked body. Jean-Claude caught her as she went down and yanked her upright. The vampire's long-dead corpse, its undead heart spilling the last of its stolen blood, turned a sick shade of gray. Leanna's heart hammered a thousand fists inside her chest as Legrand's body darkened and shriveled before her eyes.

Good, she thought fiercely. *Good.*

Then it occurred to her that Jackson's body, lying behind her, had met the same fate.

She had done that to him. She couldn't bear to look. She stared at her bloody hands instead.

"Get me out of here, Jean-Claude."

The young vampire gripped her shoulders. "Leanna—"

"Now!"

"No, you don't understand..."

"Get. Me. Out!" She balled up her fists and pounded his chest. Pain shot up her arms. It was nothing compared to the pain in her ripped and bleeding heart.

"I can't bear it. I can't stay here. I can't look at him..."

Jean-Claude shook her, hard enough to whip her head forward and back. "Leanna. Listen to me. Jackson...he's not gone."

She stilled. "What did you say?"

"Jackson is not gone."

Gently, Jean-Claude turned her. Jackson's body lay on the floor, motionless and pale. The bloody wound in his chest gaped. His arms were flung wide; his eyes were open and staring at the ceiling. He looked like the dead man he was.

A trickle of blood pulsed from his chest.

Leanna lurched out of Jean-Claude's grip. Falling on her knees, she placed both her palms over the hole in Jackson's chest. The faintest of pulses beat against her hand.

"Gods in Annwyn," she breathed. "His heart...it's still beating."

She looked up. Jean-Claude was standing over her, his outline blurry through her tears. "If that is true, the stake could not have passed through it."

"My magic..." she whispered. "It must have deflected the blow."

"Yes. If his heart had been pierced, he'd be nothing but dust. But even so...it will be some time before he can move on his own. We have to get him out of here, before—" He broke off with a curse as a muffled shout sounded behind the oak door. *"Merde.* They are here."

Leanna looked up. "Who?

Heavy fists pounded on the door. The iron latch rattled. Angry voices demanded entrance. *"Ouvrez!"* Open.

"Jean-Claude, what is it? What's happening?"

The young vampire ran to the door and stooped to gather Solange into his arms. Slowly, he backed away. "Legrand's minions know he is gone. They will break down the door to get to us. Mon Dieu! How can we fight so many?"

"But why? Legrand is gone. We mean them no harm. Why should any of them want to destroy us?"

"Because one vampire must rule Europe. Jackson Cabot was second in power to Legrand. Now he is first. But he is in no condition to defend his rank."

"You mean—any vampire who wants to be Europe's master must destroy Jackson first?"

"Or chase him off the continent."

"That should be no problem," Leanna said. "I'd guess that he's more than ready to leave."

The door shuddered on its hinges. "He will not get the chance. Not when that door gives way. They will rip him to shreds, then start in on each other."

"We've got to get out of here before that happens! Is there a back way out of this place?" She scanned the room, peering through smoke and flames. There was no second door that she could see. "A secret passage?"

"No. At least in all the time I've been held here, I have not seen evidence of one."

A mighty crash shook the door. The fused hinges groaned. Tendrils of vampire magic curled under the door, reaching for the minds within.

Jean-Claude laid Solange's body in the shelter of a heavy armoire, bending to smooth her hair from her face and place a gentle kiss on her brow before returning to stand beside Leanna. "Jackson saved my life. I will die defending him."

"Not if I can help it," Leanna muttered.

Constructing a quick barrier spell, she threw it over the door. It wouldn't hold indefinitely, not against vampire magic, but it would buy some time. Enough time, she hoped.

She turned and scanned the room, hunting through smoke and detritus, flinging dousing spells at the worst of the fire. At last, she spied a flash of silver. Her clutch purse. Snatching it up, she fumbled inside for her cell phone.

Jackson tracked her movements. "What are you doing?"

"Calling for help."

Angry voices growled on the other side of the door. "*Un, deux, trois...*" A thundering crash shook the room. Leanna stifled a cry. Dark magic and brute strength would soon shatter her barrier spell. She stabbed the phone's power button.

"What help?" Jean-Claude demanded.

Leanna, her gaze intent on the phone's display, didn't answer. "Come on..."

Searching...searching...

No service.

"Ballocks." She waved the phone in the air. "Damn. Damn, damn, *damn*. No signal. We're too far below ground." Gods, maybe Jean-Claude was right. Maybe they were doomed after all.

The door shook.

"There is a telephone," Jean-Claude said suddenly. "A—what do you call it?—a land line."

Leanna's gaze snapped to the vampire. "What?"

"A telephone. Behind that panel by the door. I do not know what good it will do, but—"

"Gods in Annwyn," Leanna gasped, lunging for her last lifeline. "Why didn't you say that in the first place?"

She snatched the receiver off the hook just as the doors top hinge cracked.

Chapter Fifteen

Leanna bypassed Mac's number and went straight to Christine's. It was Kalen's magic she needed, but she knew the Immortal put as much distance as possible between himself and modern technology. He'd rather be roasted alive than carry a cell phone.

Thankfully, his wife answered hers on the first ring. "Leanna? Goddess, what's wrong? We thought you'd gone to a spa in Tuscany…"

"No. Actually, I'm in a spot of trouble…"

Kalen arrived even before Leanna had finished her terse explanation, his broad form materializing out of the smoky dungeon air. Immediately the room seemed smaller.

Jean-Claude's eyes nearly bugged out of his head.

The Immortal took a quick survey of the room. Leanna winced, imagining the scene through his eyes. It looked bad, very bad. Death and death magic. Blood. Vampires. And—dear gods, she'd completely forgotten until that very instant—she was stark naked.

Kalen fixed her with a baleful glare. "Leanna—"

He broke off as a crash splintered a corner of the door. Leanna's barrier spell spiderwebbed. Scowling fiercely, Kalen held up one hand, reinforcing Leanna's magic.

"Just what kind of trouble have you gotten yourself into this time?"

Jean-Claude made a choking sound. "Mon Dieu. You're...you're..."

"Kalen," Leanna told him. "One of the Immortals who saved the world a couple years back. He'll get us out. One at a time. He'll take Solange first, then you. Then Jackson."

Kalen's voice dripped warning. "Leanna. Surely you did not just offer my magical services to vampires?"

"Yes, Kalen, that's exactly what I did. And that pile of dust over there? That's a really nasty vampire I just staked. His rabid minions are on the verge of knocking down the door. There's no time to explain more. Just trust me—"

"To do what? Stay away from death magic? Stay out of vamp clubs? Stop killing? What the hell happened to the vows you took in Annwyn? Were they nothing but a pack of lies? No—" He cut off her reply with a second raised hand. "Don't even bother answering. It's Mac you'll need to explain yourself to."

She wasn't sure what frightened her more—the thought of facing her demigod brother or the ferocious growls on the other side of the dungeon door. Jean-Claude went paler than the pale he already was. The melted hinges creaked ominously.

"Kalen," Leanna ground out. "Shut up! Lecture me later. There's no time for it now."

The Immortal grabbed for her wrist. "All right. Let's get you out of here."

She eluded his grasp. "No! I mean—yes, we need to get out, but...you've got to take the others out first."

"You mean these vampires? And that unconscious death witch? You have got to be kidding me. This is their world. Let them deal with it."

"No. You don't understand. This isn't just any vampire club. It belongs—belonged—to Armand Legrand."

Kalen inhaled sharply. "Europe's vampire master?"

"The same." She jerked her chin to the dusty pile of leather on the floor. "That's all that's left of him."

The Immortal's brows shot up. "How in the name of all eternity did you manage that?"

"We'll chat later, Kalen. Right now, could you just please shut up get Jean-Claude and his wife out of here?"

"Solange first," Jean-Claude said as the cracks in the door splintered and widened. He thrust his wife into Kalen's arms. His shoulders went back as he met the Immortal's gaze. "Please."

Kalen muttered something under his breath and winked out of existence, taking Solange with him.

Leanna's shoulders sagged. "Thank the gods."

She threw all her magic into holding the door. In the space of half a dozen heartbeats, Kalen was back.

"Christine's speechless," he reported. "And believe me, that doesn't happen often. As for Mac...well, I'd rather not repeat Mac's exact words."

"Jean-Claude next," was all Leanna said.

Kalen placed his hand on the young vampire's shoulder and disappeared a second time. Leanna's gaze found Jackson. He hadn't moved an inch. He looked so pale, so still. So...dead.

He was dead. He was vampire. He'd never be otherwise.

Kalen reappeared at her elbow.

"You next."

"No. Take Jackson," she said, blinking back tears.

Kalen's charcoal-gray eyes rested briefly on Jackson's still figure. "Who is he?"

"A...friend. I knew him a century ago. When he was still alive."

"You care for him."

"Yes. I did then and I do now."

"Leanna. He's a vampire. A creature of death."

"Damn it, Kalen, don't you think I know that?"

"Un, deux, trois..."

The battering ram crashed against the door. The room shook from the force of the impact. Death magic surged. Leanna clutched Kalen's arm. Gods. Legrand's minions would take the whole building down at this rate.

"Just get him out of here!"

Kalen nodded. Kneeling, he placed his hand on Jackson's arm. "I'll be back in three seconds."

An instant later, they were gone. Leanna released a long stream of air from her lungs.

Before she could draw her next breath, the dungeon door shattered.

Chapter Sixteen

"Gods damn it, that was too close."

Kalen uttered another few choice words as he dumped Leanna on a chair in the sitting room of his hotel suite. "If I had arrived one second later, you'd have been nothing but a collection of bloody body parts strewn across the floor."

Leanna, eyes squeezed shut, could only nod at Kalen's rage. Her heart was racing and her lungs were in the midst of a hard spasm. A verbal reply was totally beyond possibility.

A second angry male voice intruded. "Bloody hell, Leanna. What in the name of Annwyn were you doing in Armand Legrand's club?"

"Mac, back off. Can't you see she's in shock?" The admonition came from Mac's wife, Artemis.

Artemis tugged her to her feet. Leanna stumbled after her. Dimly, she was aware of her sister-in-law pushing her into the shower and washing her like a child. Stepping out of the water, she felt a whisper of silk descend on her shoulders. A robe. She wrapped it around her body and pulled the sash tight.

When she stepped back into the sitting room, the first thing she saw was Mac. Gods. Her brother looked angry enough to tear someone limb from limb. Leanna had a pretty good idea who was first on his list of candidates.

Artemis blocked his approach. "Now, Mac, get a grip..."

"Grip, nothing! She deserves a good shaking. Kalen found her up to her ears in death magic."

The disappointment in Mac's eyes hurt Leanna like hell. Gods, there was so much to answer for. And she would answer. But right now...

"Where's Jackson?"

Mac swore.

"Both vampires and their death witch are in the master suite," Kalen, standing by the window, cut in. "Christine is with them. I warned her not to waste too much of her magic on them, especially the vampires. They'll heal fast enough on their own."

Leanna rose on shaky feet and headed toward the closed door Kalen indicated. Mac stepped up, blocking her path.

"You swore to me, Leanna. You swore to Niniane. Bugger it all, you swore on Annwyn's silver tree of life that you would give up death magic!"

"I know. And I'm sorry. But...I just couldn't turn away. Not from Jackson."

"What is this vamp to you, Leanna?"

"Please. I'll explain it all later. Right now—I just need to see him."

Artemis none-too-subtly tugged Mac out of Leanna's way. "Let your sister be. Can't you see how upset she is? Whoever—whatever—the man is, she's in love with him."

Mac frowned as Leanna shoved passed him. Christine, her blue eyes grave, slipped from the bedroom as Leanna approached the door.

"Good luck," she mouthed as she caught Leanna's eye.

Leanna steeled herself and opened the door. The room was dark, the heavy drapes drawn against the encroaching dawn. Jackson lay in the center of the large bed, eyes closed, his face almost as pale as the bed linens. His chest was bare. The ugly wound she'd inflicted on him gaped open. The jagged skin around it was ripped and raw.

"He is weak," a woman's low voice said. "He needs blood to heal completely. But he will survive."

Leanna's gaze swung to Solange. She sat in a deep armchair, awake and alert, clad in a white terry cloth robe that matched her pallor. Jean-Claude, newly showered and similarly garbed, stood behind her.

"Thank the gods for that," Leanna said.

"Jackson may curse those same gods, when he awakens," Solange replied.

"But why? Legrand is gone."

Solange shivered and looked away. Jean-Claude regarded Leanna with sober eyes. "My wife means to say that...our master's existence, for so long, has been fed by little more than his hatred of Legrand. Now that Legrand is gone..." He spread his hands in a gesture of helplessness. "We cannot say what Jackson will be. What he will do. How he will live."

"Whatever happens," Leanna said, "He won't have to face it alone. I'll be with him."

"Be careful what you promise," Jean-Claude said. "It is not easy, being the living companion of a vampire." His eyes, troubled, fell on Solange.

"I never imagined it was," Leanna said. "But someone will have to take the job. It's not fair to ask Solange to guard two vampires. Jackson needs a steward of his own, one with very powerful magic."

"Are you truly willing to take on that responsibility?" Solange asked.

"Yes. Yes, I am." Her gaze strayed back to Jackson. "Do you think he will agree?"

Solange shrugged and looked away.

"Your life magic friends won't like it," Jean-Claude warned.

Leanna rubbed her arms. "Likely, that's true. But I don't care. I love Jackson."

"Do you? I know what you did to the master long ago, in Paris. You are the reason Jackson is vampire." He paused. "He has hated you for a very long time."

"I know I have much to atone for, if only he'll let me." She blinked back a blur of tears. "Please. May I...may I be alone with him?"

Reluctantly, Jean-Claude helped Solange to her feet. "But of course," he said.

Then he let out a reluctant chuckle, and Leanna caught a glimpse of the living man he'd once been. "In the meantime, my wife and I will endeavor to pass the time of day with your appalled friends."

***

"Jackson? Can you hear me?"

The woman's voice was low and sweet, and sounded like a dream he wished would never end. Jackson muttered a noncommittal sound and slipped deeper into velvet darkness.

Wet heat on his cheek. Soft lips, caressing his temple.

The woman spoke again. She was closer now. Trembling.

For him?

"Jackson, please. Wake up."

He struggled to understand. He thought the voice came from his past—a past he tried never to think about. Such thoughts were too painful. They had the power to destroy. For years, decades, a century, he'd locked them away. Why had this siren come to awaken those fatal yearnings?

The voice moved away. The woman's heat retreated, leaving him chilled. He suppressed the urge to call her back. He didn't deserve her. He—

Cold, wet shock assaulted him. Icy water, like a slap across his face. He sputtered, jerking upright, gasping for breath. His eyes snapped open, just in time to be blinded by a second liquid assault.

"Thank the gods," she said. "That's much better."

He wiped the back of his hand across his eyes, blinking furiously. He lay on a wide, soft bed; he was naked beneath the cool linens. His chest ached. How had he gotten here? The last thing he remembered was Leanna looming over him, driving a wooden stake into his heart.

She loomed over him again now. This time, her weapon of choice was a chilled bottle of mineral water.

He shoved aside the soaked sheet and swung his legs over the side of the bed. The room lurched unpleasantly.

He glared at her. "Why the hell are you trying to drown me?"

She set the bottle on the nightstand with a dull thud. Belatedly, he realized her hand was shaking. Tears leaking from her eyes.

She dashed them away with the back of her hand. "I'm sorry, Jackson. But...seeing you so pale and still, with that ugly hole in your chest... Gods. You looked...dead."

"I am dead."

She hugged her torso. "You know what I mean."

He peered down at his wound. The movement of his eyes caused black squiggles to dance in his vision. He felt lightheaded. Weak as a newborn kitten. And hungry. Ravenous, in fact. His wound cried for blood. Healing, nourishing blood.

And the sweetest meal he could ever wish for was within arm's reach.

He couldn't let himself think about that. "Your aim is pathetic," he said. "My heart is at least an inch to the right."

She didn't laugh. "I know that! Oh, gods, Jackson, I tried so hard to miss entirely. One inch was all my magic could do."

"It was enough, it seems."

"But you lost so much blood. It was everywhere. And now...you need more before you'll begin to heal."

Blood.

He couldn't prevent his gaze from seeking and finding the delicate pulse point on Leanna's neck. He could hear her Sidhe blood, vibrant with life, rushing through her veins. Despite his weakened state, lust stirred. He curled his fingers on the edge of the mattress so he wouldn't reach for her.

Scowling, he looked around the room for the first time. "Where are we?"

"My hotel. This is Kalen and Christine's suite, actually. Mac and Kalen—and their wives—are in the next room. I called Kalen from Legrand's club. He's able to translocate at will, you know. It's one of his magical talents." She was babbling, Jackson thought incredulously. He'd never witnessed that before.

"He got us out of Legrand's dungeon, and brought us all here. To the hotel. You, me, Solange, Jean-Claude...."

Jackson's memory of recent events was elusive. "Solange..." he began. He thought she'd been gravely injured. "Will she live?"

"Oh, yes! Certainly. Christine's cast some potent healing spells and they seem to be working fine. Solange is awake and Jean-Claude is with her. They're in the other bedroom." She grimaced. "With Mac and Kalen."

"Jean-Claude is well?"

"His physical wounds have almost completely healed, at least." She hesitated. "After all he's been through, regaining his emotional health will probably take some time."

Regrettably, the scene in Legrand's dungeon was becoming clearer in Jackson's memory. He nodded grimly. "Vampires are a strong breed. You needn't fear Jean-Claude and I will hide behind you and your friends. All three of us will leave this place at sunset. Legrand will surely be searching—"

"Legrand isn't searching. He's...he's nothing but dust now."

It took a moment for her statement to register in his mind. When it did, for a moment he could do nothing but stare.

"Dust?" Jackson said finally. "But how? He defeated me. Who could possibly have killed him? Kalen?"

"No. He went down before Kalen arrived on the scene. It was me, Jackson. I destroyed Legrand."

"You, Leanna?" Jackson felt as though he'd been punched in the gut. "God damn it, did you have sex with that monster after all? While I lay unconscious at your feet?"

"No!" she said quickly. "Gods, no. I swear. I got rid of Legrand the old-fashioned way. I staked him. With the same stake I drove through your chest, actually."

"How? Legrand's power..."

"I'm not sure how I did it. After I impaled you, Legrand stood there laughing, gloating. It was horrible—I thought I'd pierced your heart. I thought you were gone. My mind blanked—I went insane, I think, with rage. I barely remember what happened after that, but somehow I yanked the stake from your body and lunged at Legrand. I...I must have caught him by surprise. The stake went clean through his heart."

"My God." Legrand, destroyed? At Leanna's hand? After all Jackson's years of carnal self-deprivation and careful planning? An ironic twist indeed. He fell silent, absorbing the enormity of the notion. Legrand. Gone.

It would take some time to get used to.

He felt Leanna's gaze drop to the hole in his chest.

"Does it hurt?"

"It will heal," he said.

She sighed and sank down next to him on the bed. She was too close. His fingers were just inches from her pulse. If he moved his hand slightly, he could grasp her wrist and bring it to his lips.

Blood-hunger gnawed his gut. He ached to bury his fangs in her sweet flesh. Bury his hard cock in her body. Fool that he was, he didn't even care that only a flimsy door separated him from the combined wrath of a demigod, an Immortal warrior, and their two witchy wives.

Damn it. Didn't Leanna realize the danger he represented? He spoke through gritted teeth. "You may leave me now. I am fine."

Leanna's brows rose. "Fine? Who are you kidding? Fine is the last thing you look. Death warmed over is a more apt description." She bit her lip.

The innocent, erotic nibble went straight to his groin. He stifled a groan.

She gasped. "Jackson? What is it? Are you weak? Do you need blood?"

"No," he ground out. "No. I don't need blood. Not your blood, at any rate. I only need you to leave me alone. Get out of here, Leanna. Go back to your life-magic friends."

The perverse woman didn't obey. Instead, she laid her delicate hand on his chest, her palm covering his wound. His fingers closed on her wrist. God help him, he didn't have the strength to push her away.

Her mouth brushed his jaw.

"Leanna. Don't do this. You'll regret it."

"I won't."

She nuzzled him with her cheek. Stretching her neck, she offered her pulse to him. Her blood beat against his lips. Tantalizing. Forbidden.

Hunger and lust exploded; his fangs emerged. He opened his mouth to mutter a soft curse. The tips of his incisors scored her skin.

"I'm willing, Jackson, and you can't turn me vampire. Why hesitate?"

"If I lose control I could easily drain your veins dry."

"You won't lose control. I trust you, Jackson. Utterly. I love you, Jackson. My blood is yours. Whatever you need from me, I'm ready to give."

Gods. She just didn't understand. She was light and life; he was death. They didn't belong together. Nevertheless, his throat burned with painful need; his cock throbbed mercilessly. Her pulse beat against his lips. One bite and she would be his. Forever.

"Make love to me," she whispered.

"Leanna..."

She lifted her head from his shoulder. He felt the loss of contact keenly, but didn't pull her back.

"Is it because you think you'll lose the power you worked so long to gain? Because if—"

"No. Not that," he said. "I gathered that magic for one purpose. To defeat Legrand. Now that he is gone..."

"There's no reason to push me away."

He expelled a rush of air from his lungs. "Leanna, you don't know what you're offering! Do you honestly think that if I make love to you now, and drink your blood, that I could ever let you go? If I take you now, I'll never be strong enough to set you free."

She smiled with all the brilliance of the sun he'd not seen in a century. "I don't want to be free of you. I want to stay by your side, always. Solange will have her hands full watching after Jean-Claude—you can't expect her to guard two vampires. You need a new steward. I'm the perfect choice."

He stared at her, aghast. "You can't mean that! You're Sidhe, Leanna. Your kind doesn't consort with vampires. Sidhe are creatures of light."

"Actually, I'm more of a night person."

"Don't joke. I'm serious. It's preposterous. A Sidhe cannot be a vampire's steward."

"Why not?" She placed a kiss on his jaw.

He groaned. When she did that, he couldn't quite remember why not. In fact, he couldn't seem to stop himself from reaching for her. Her blood called to him, filling his ears with a low, deep buzz. He struggled to form a coherent sentence.

"You'd have to live in caves. Caverns. Dank cellars."

She kissed him again. "Sidhe love the earth."

"Vampire society is highly territorial. We'll never be left in peace. I'll be threatened by rivals, always. You'll be in constant battle with their stewards."

Her lips grazed the corner of his mouth. "My magic is up to the challenge, I believe."

"Your brother...your friends...they'll be horrified."

"True," she agreed. "In fact, they already are. But I don't care."

She nibbled his lips. Her breasts squashed between their bodies. He swept his hand up her side and filled his palm with their soft, yielding bounty.

She licked him, the tip of her tongue scraping from his chin to his ear. "Gods, Jackson, you taste so good."

It was too much. With a groan of surrender, he rolled her beneath him on the bed and plundered her mouth. His fangs scraped her lip, slid over her jaw. He scored a thin line down her neck, then pressed his incisors to her throbbing pulse.

Her robe fell open. Gods, she was naked beneath it. She wrapped her legs around his waist. The fullness of his erection slid between her thighs.

"Come into me, Jackson."

Even if he'd wanted to, he couldn't have stopped himself from obeying. Dragging in a breath, he bit deep, his fangs sinking into her neck at the exact instant he pushed himself into her body. Her blood was sweet on his tongue; her inner muscles clenched his shaft in an intoxicating embrace.

He fed as he moved inside her. Euphoria beyond imagining tossed him high. Leanna's blood was potent, magical; her love was his renewal. Life essence and life magic spread through his limbs, into his veins, his muscle, his sinew. He felt the wound in his chest close completely as he filled his hands with her body and his heart and soul with her love.

They exploded together, in a shower of peace so profound that when the world stopped spinning and Jackson's sanity finally returned, he found his face wet with tears.

"You've done it now," he whispered, his arms tightening around her. "I'll never let you go."

Leanna snuggled closer, smiling. She didn't open her eyes.

"Good," she said.

Epilogue

The nice thing about February on the north coast of Scotland was that the sun barely rose above the horizon, and then only for scant hours each day. That happy fact of nature made the Immortal Kalen's island castle the perfect vampire winter home.

Leanna, wineglass in hand, glanced across the library at Jackson. A casual observer would never guess he was vampire. In the six months since they'd left Rome, Jackson had lost much of the pallor most people associated with vampires. Her rich Sidhe blood had done that for him. Her husband no longer hunted human blood.

As for Jackson's vampire power—true, his magic wasn't increasing at same amazing rate it had during his years of celibacy, but it wasn't draining, either, as they'd feared. The potent Sidhe life essence in Leanna's blood more than made up for any deficits. Even better, Leanna had come to realize the pleasure she drew from her relationship with Jackson had nothing to do with her past death magic addiction and everything to do with love. Leanna offered Jackson the inspirational benefits of her muse magic along with her blood, while he offered her all the love he had to give. They no longer feared their magic would harm each other. On the contrary, their mutual love only strengthened them.

Inspired by Leanna, Jackson had resumed his long-abandoned artistic explorations. He painted and sculpted almost every spare moment he wasn't worshipping Leanna in bed. Against all odds, she'd helped Jackson find something he'd believed was lost to him forever. Happiness. He'd regained the exuberant good humor that had drawn her in Paris. He teased her and laughed often. In a few months, when the Scottish summer days began to stretch to unmanageable lengths, they would travel south and spend a blissfully dark winter in Patagonia. Leanna was looking forward to the trip. She'd never seen a penguin in its natural habitat.

Solange and Jean-Claude would be traveling with them. Leanna knew Jackson was worried about Jean-Claude. He'd been slow in healing from his ordeal as Legrand's slave and uncomfortable in adapting to a vampire existence with his wife as his protector. It would take some time for Jackson's former steward to come to terms with everything that had happened. In the meantime, Solange was doing everything in her power to speed her husband's recovery.

Leanna sent Jackson a nervous smile. He paused in his conversation with Kalen—they were deeply engrossed in a discussion of Impressionism—and sent her an encouraging grin in return. The sight was almost enough to dispel the cold knot of anxiety in her chest.

Almost.

She took a deep, almost desperate sip of merlot.

"Gods," she muttered under her breath. "What I really need is some good Scots whiskey. A whole barrel of it."

Mac, standing at her elbow, chuckled. "That's precisely why Kalen locked up his Glenfiddich."

Christine and Artemis exchanged amused glances. Leanna scowled.

"Don't worry." Christine, ever the peacemaker, patted Leanna's arm. "I'm sure everything will be fine."

"Fine?" Leanna demanded. "Fine? How could it possibly be fine?" She poked a finger at Mac. "This meeting is not a good idea. I can't believe I let you talk me into it."

"Relax, love." Mac looked calm enough, his arm casually draped over his wife's shoulders, but Leanna could tell he was nearly as keyed up as she was.

"It's only our mother, after all," he said wryly. "And you must admit, Niniane does have the right to meet her only son-in-law."

"She's going to explode," Leanna said flatly.

Mac grinned. "Likely. But look at the bright side. Mum will be forced to admit Artemis isn't the worst thing to happen to the family. A vampire is clearly a worse in-law than a reformed death witch."

Artemis rolled her eyes. "Thanks, Mac."

"Go ahead," Leanna said darkly. "Make jokes. It won't save you when Niniane gets here."

Niniane may have acknowledged Leanna, but it had only been at Mac's insistence. Leanna's relationship with her mother was shaky at best. And now that Leanna had broken the vows she'd made in Annwyn and married a vampire to boot...

She sent a worried glance toward the far side of the library, where Artemis's older son, Zander, sprawled on the floor with his infant half-brother, Cameron, and Christine's and Kalen's immortal toddler, Ellie.

"I'm not sure it's safe, having the children in here when Niniane arrives. Maybe Pearl should watch them somewhere else."

"It'll be safer with them here, actually," Mac replied, his gaze resting fondly on his first-born, who at the moment was sprawled on his pudgy stomach, nearsightedly surveying Kalen's Persian carpet for edible lint. "Niniane would never endanger her only grandson."

"Where is she, anyway? She should have been here by now."

Mac laughed. "So now you're anxious for old mum to arrive?"

"I'm anxious for her to come and go," Leanna muttered. "As quickly as possible."

She drew a sharp inhale as Kalen's stout Halfling/gnome housekeeper, Pearl, waddled through the library doorway. The expression on her hairy face could not have been more sour.

"May I present—"

Pearl's voice dripped with more sarcasm than Leanna thought could safely fit into the room.

"—Her Royal Highness, Sidhe Queen of Annwyn, Revered Keeper of Celtic Mysteries, High Counselor of the Sidhe Court, Honored Protector of Celtic Lore, Most Beautiful and Benevolent Benefactress of Celtic Creatures in Annwyn and in the Human World..."

Mac snorted under his breath, then covered the laugh with a cough when Artemis elbowed him in the ribs.

"...Niniane the Exquisite!"

Pearl looked like she wanted to vomit.

Leanna thought she might spew as well.

Instead, she held her breath and pasted a smile on her face as Niniane glided through the door. Her mother's youthful beauty was, as always, stunning. The Sidhe queen may have been well over a thousand years old, but she looked no more aged than a twenty-two-year-old human female. Her gown, a stunning confection woven from silver leaves, dewdrops, and pink petals, draped a perfect, dainty body. Platinum blond hair, braided into a regal crown atop her head, accented her long, graceful neck and delicately pointed ears.

Dimly, Leanna was aware of Jackson moving to her side and cupping her elbow. "Don't forget to breathe," he whispered.

Leanna inhaled.

Mac reached Niniane first. Bending, he kissed her cheek.

"Hullo, Mum. You're looking lovely, as always. So glad you could make it."

"Where is he, Mackie?" Niniane demanded, her eyes sweeping the library. "Where is this—" She gave a theatric shudder, "—*vampire* your sister's married?"

Icy fingers of apprehension clutched Leanna's throat and squeezed. She didn't care what Mac said. This was an exceedingly bad idea. Niniane was liable to eviscerate Jackson. She was more than capable of doing it, right here in Kalen's library, without harming a hair on the children's heads.

Jackson shook off the death grip Leanna had on his arm. Smiling, he approached Niniane and bowed.

"Arthur Jackson Cabot IV, at your service, your Highness."

Niniane's mulish expression didn't flicker as she gave Jackson a blatant once-over.

She huffed and met Leanna's gaze across the room. "This man hardly looks like a vampire."

"He's—" Leanna began.

"It's your lovely daughter's influence that keeps me so...alive," Jackson cut in. "Nevertheless, I assure you, I am vampire."

"And I don't have a glamour on him, either," Leanna said.

Her mother cast her a quelling glance. "I know that."

Jackson graced his mother-in-law with a flash of his fangs. Niniane gazed at him a moment, then sniffed and continued to address her daughter.

"So he looks like a living human. That hardly matters. It's just not natural, a Sidhe married to a death creature. It was bad enough Mac took up with a death witch of such scandalous ancestry—"

"Mother—" Mac cut in, his tone ominous.

Niniane huffed. "—but at least my darling daughter-in-law is alive and practices only life magic now." She sent a brilliant smile toward the children. "I must admit, Artemis has given me a lovely grandson. But vampires? They're pure death, Leanna. And they can't reproduce."

"My apologies, your Highness," Jackson said mildly.

Niniane ignored him.

Leanna let out a huff. Handing her wine glass to Christine, she stalked to Jackson's side.

"Mother, stop it. Right now. I won't tolerate you being rude to my husband."

"Leanna. I know I treated you poorly for most of your life. But I thought we'd gotten past that. I accepted you into Annwyn. I acknowledged you as my daughter. In return, you swore you would abandon death magic forever. And *this* is how you repay me? With an undead son-in-law?"

"It had nothing to do with you, Mother! I married Jackson because I love him."

"Your Highness," Jackson interjected. "May I speak?"

Niniane's brows arched toward her hairline. She turned and fixed Jackson with a baleful stare.

Leanna held her breath at her husband's breech of Sidhe etiquette. Humans, even undead ones, did not pose direct, uninvited questions to Sidhe royalty. A long pause ensued, in which even Mac shifted nervously. Then Kalen cleared his throat in subtle warning.

Niniane rolled her eyes. "Go ahead. Speak."

Leanna let out a long breath.

"I love your daughter," Jackson began. "And she loves me. Her life magic balances my death magic. I will honor and defend her with every breath in my unfortunately undead body. There is only one flaw in our happiness. Leanna wishes her mother's blessing on our union. Please, will you give it?"

For a long moment, the room breathed in silence. Even the babies ceased babbling. The only sound came from the ormolu clock on the mantle. The precise ticking fell on Leanna's ears like blows of a hammer on an anvil.

Her heart nearly seized when Jackson reached for Niniane's hand. A warning spark of elfshot fired from the queen's fingers. Jackson smiled as if he hadn't noticed.

Bowing, he brushed a kiss across the backs of Niniane's fingers. "Please, my lady. Give Leanna your blessing. Then her happiness will be as perfect as you are."

Mac made a choking sound. "Laying it on a bit thick, no?" Leanna heard her brother whisper to his wife.

"Shut up," Artemis hissed back at him.

Niniane tilted her head back and examined Jackson's face. "You're a charming devil, aren't you? And handsome, too. No wonder Leanna tossed her better judgment to the four winds."

"Quite right," Jackson replied.

The queen's perfect bosom rose and fell in an exaggerated sigh. "My standards, I fear, are dropping to new depths. I suppose I should count myself lucky Leanna didn't bring home a demon. At least you used to be alive."

Jackson quirked his most endearing smile. "Does this mean we may have your blessing?"

Niniane made an impatient gesture. "Oh yes, all right, you may have it. All I want is my daughter's happiness, after all."

"Brava, Mum," Mac murmured. "You do have a heart, after all. Who'd have thought?"

"Oh, Mother..." Leanna could hardly get the words past the sudden lump burning in her throat. She wiped away a tear. "Thank you. Thank you so much."

"Yes," Jackson echoed, his arm tight around Leanna's waist. "Thank you, dear Mother."

Niniane's eyes widened in pure, abject horror. *"What* did you call me?"

Jackson grinned. "'Mother,' of course. You don't mind, do you? 'Your Highness' seems far too formal for close family."

The expression on Niniane's face was priceless. "Now, let's not get carried away! My standards haven't plummeted quite so far as all that..."

Absurdly, Leanna began to laugh.

Mac's chuckle joined her. A moment later, Kalen, Christine, and Artemis joined in. The babies giggled. Pearl added a husky guffaw.

Eventually, even Niniane smiled.

"Well done, Mum," Mac said, wrapping his mother in a tight hug. "See? That wasn't so hard, was it?"

"You have no idea," Niniane muttered. "Thank the gods I only had two children. Now," she added, looking toward the children. "I want to hold Cameron."

Jackson kissed Leanna soundly on the lips as Niniane glided toward her grandson. "See? I told you everything would be perfect."

"Hmm..." Leanna tilted her head and pretended to consider the situation. "You did, didn't you?"

He nodded. "Most certainly."

Leanna smiled up at Jackson.

His eyes laughed down at her.

And the moment was, indeed, perfect.

Thank You

Thank you for reading *Blood Debt*. I hope you enjoyed it! Would you like to know when my next book is available? There are a few ways you can keep in touch:

Sign up for my newsletter at joynash.com

Visit me on social media:
facebook.com/joynash/
twitter: @joynashauthor
joynash.blogspot.com

Now, turn the page to read an excerpt from

The Night Everything Fell Apart
The Nephilim: Book One
Available Now!

joynash.com
excerpts, extras, behind-the-book secrets

The Night Everything Fell Apart
The Nephilim: Book One

*Available now
in paperback and ebook*

Arthur Camulus couldn't say it felt good to be back in England. To be honest, it felt like crap. And wasn't that bloody ironic? He'd spent years plotting his return.

At least, he thought he had.

Why was he here? He couldn't remember. His brain was that fucked up. It'd been hours, or days, or maybe even weeks, since he'd emerged from his Ordeal. Heat consumed his body; every nerve ending was ablaze. Opal lights moved under his skin. Stray sparks shot from his fingertips. He swiped his tongue across the roof of his mouth. His spit tasted of metal. He stunk of sweat and worse. If he looked down at his bare chest, he'd see blood.

Not his own blood. That much, he was certain of.

The first time his body had changed, the pain had been nearly unendurable. The second shift had been easier. His flesh was adjusting to its new condition. His mind? Fried. Horrors flashed behind his eyes. Shouts rang in his ears. The magic was his and yet it wasn't. He couldn't call it with any consistency or direct it once it responded.

He needed help.

The night was heavy with fog. How long until dawn? Hard to tell. Clouds obscured moon and stars. Night mist soaked his skin as he flew. Moorland, mottled with shadows, peeked through the haze below. To his newly-gained night vision, everything appeared strangely rendered in shades of gray and green.

It was difficult to keep steady long enough to orient himself. His wings were more awkward than he'd anticipated. Right and left refused to cooperate. Flight was dodgy.

The site was the highest point for miles around. Even so, he only just managed to see past its protective wardings. He landed inelegantly, in a neglected garden. Here, the fog was thinner, sound muted. The old manor rose like a ghost, its windows like so many vacant eyes. He tilted his head and knew a rush of relief. There might be gaps—vast gaps—in the quagmire of his memory, but this place, at least, occupied solid ground.

Tŷ'r Cythraul. House of the Demon.

He willed his wings to melt into his back. Surprisingly, they obeyed. The lights under his skin faded. Breath hissed between his teeth as his body relaxed into human form.

His childhood home was an unassuming structure. Square and stolid, with a gray stone face. Four rooms below, five above. The attic, one large space under a steeply sloping roof, had once been Arthur's domain. His life here had been happy until that last, horrific night.

The front door—solid oak, polished to a high sheen—

simultaneously beckoned and repulsed. Reluctant to face it, he pivoted, taking in the garden and its encircling stone wall, where his mother, in all her varied moods, had spent hours tending her plants. Now weeds overran the paths, feral herbs wrestled with gangly shrubs, and saplings choked the well pump.

Only the oak was unchanged. Its trunk, so massive that three men with outstretched arms could not have encircled it, stood near one corner of the house. Moss-covered roots spread out around the base like a treacherous welcome mat. Branches stretched over the roof, the tips scratching the slates.

I've come for the oak. With sudden clarity, the memory of it burst upon him.

Funny thing about memories. When they weren't your own, they had no context. Bits and pieces of his ancestors' lives churned about in Arthur's skull, like so much tornado-tossed debris. So many events, so many images. So many lost emotions. A thousand films playing at once, reeling past too quickly to absorb.

A dull ache pounded his forehead. He bowed his head and pressed his fingertips against it. *The oak,* he reminded himself. *The oak. What the bloody hell was he supposed to remember about the oak?*

Violent as lightning, one memory, one single lucid thought, flashed through his brain. He sucked in air. His eyes flew open. A morass of emotions—clawing, sucking, sickening—swamped him. He stumbled toward the oak and laid his left hand on its trunk.

Power leapt like a rabid dog. Too much, too strong: he

couldn't control it. The magic savaged his brain, mauled his skull. Lifted his mind from his body. Desperately, he focused on the wood under his palm. He couldn't fail in this. He *would* not.

He swept his hand downward. The bark warmed. The ancient wood went soft. His fingers sank into it. Something slipped into his hand. He pulled the object out of the wood. Several seconds passed as he gathered the courage to look at it.

When at last he did, he knew. Who he was. What he was.

Arthur Camulus. Human. Demon.

Nephil.

And he knew one more thing: he was in deep, deep shit.

The ancestors of King Arthur
guard the magic of Camelot

The Druids of Avalon
Joy Nash

Celtic Fire

Rhiannon's loyalties are split between her clan and the Roman soldier who has captured her heart.

The Grail King

A mysterious cup and the Roman woman searching for it hold the key to Owein's future.

Deep Magic

Gwen and Marcus are consumed by forces beyond their control as together they forge Excalibur.

Silver Silence

Rhys travels into the future to find Breena in the company of a wily old Druid whose magic and methods feel disturbingly familiar.

Enter the World of
The Immortals

USA Today Bestselling Series

Immortals Books by Joy Nash

The Awakening

A light witch travels to the Scottish Highlands to convince a cynical Immortal Warrior to join the fight for the survival of the human race.

The Crossing

A Celtic demigod descends into the depths of Hell to rescue the soul of a dark witch's child.

Blood Debt

Upon escape from a century of enslavement, a tortured vampire vows to take his revenge on the beautiful Celtic *Sidhe* who killed him.

About the Author

Joy Nash is a USA Today Bestselling Author and RITA Award Finalist applauded by Booklist for her "tart wit, superbly crafted characters, and sexy, magic-steeped plots."

When Joy was seven years old, she read a book about a girl who lived on the moon. She thought it was real until her big sister came along and messed up the story with the truth. Ever since, Joy's been of the opinion that fiction is way more interesting than reality.

Joy credits her love of tortured heroes to the Brontë sisters, her fascination with magical adventure to J.R.R. Tolkien, and her weakness for snarky humor to Douglas Adams.

Connect with Joy

facebook.com/joynash/
twitter: @joynashauthor
joynash.blogspot.com

May the stories never end!

Printed in Great Britain
by Amazon